T0161063

OPERATION
BOB DYLAN'S BELT

A Jake Randall Detective Novel

OPERATION
BOB DYLAN'S BELT

Linn Wyllie

Clovercroft Publishing

PROLOGUE

A revelation can come to a man in mysterious ways. I had one came to me one foggy morning alongside a canal on a lonely stretch of an Everglades highway. The narrow road is straight, long, and desolate, paralleled on either side by deep water canals.

The red pickup truck was on its side fully submerged in the canal, the passenger side door embedded in the muddy bottom. Three rectangular yellow sheets dotted the grass and reeds along the bank. Sheriff's divers were stowing their scuba gear as the tow truck dragged the pickup up out of the murky water. A large alligator watched from just a dozen yards away. He was just waiting for us to leave. He had been here before. Somebody's plans definitely got interrupted one night a day or so ago. It happens. Frequently. Without warning. Nobody wakes up in the morning and says, "I'm gonna die today." Well, maybe terrorists and suicide bombers do. Sane and stable people don't. I'd investigated car wrecks before, all twisted metal and shattered lives. Wasn't fun. This one was different. The image kept running through my head. I could literally see it in my mind's eye. How it happened. The right rear tire coming off the pavement and onto the grassy shoulder, the driver overcorrecting, the splash as the truck twisted into a half flip and hit the still, dark water of the canal, the headlights fading into the murky depths, and finally the passenger door window coming to a stop pressed against the muddy bottom. The cab filling with black swamp water. The desperation and panic of those poor souls inside. Didn't know they could get out. From panic maybe. I don't know. Or maybe they were knocked around and dazed and just didn't even try.

The revelation came in knowing I'd need to find another line of work, more in keeping with the Buddhist-Christian-Pantheist philosopher that I am. That revelation came with the mental comparison I was making as I watching the retrieval of the red four-wheeled watery coffin. And it was a simple comparison too. I was alive in the universe of being, and these poor waterlogged corpses under the yellow sheets were not. And I wanted to stay that way. For a good long while.

"How long they been in the water?" I asked that. But didn't really want to know.

"A day. Maybe two at most. Gator got most of the fourth one. We think that was a child."

"Oh, Christ."

Deputy Frank Sanchez, my partner, nodded at my prayer and looked away. I looked up at the gator there in the canal, his head above water, at his unblinking eyes. It suddenly just pissed me off. Not the bang-your-fist-on the-table kind of pissed; and not the kick-the-dog kind of pissed. It was a rage arising from cosmic injustice kind of pissed. I drew my service pistol and fired twice at the vile, primitive beast. Double tap. Both rounds struck home. One of my few virtues is I shoot well. Very well. The gator rolled once, red froth in the splash, and sank out of sight. Two .45 rounds wouldn't necessarily kill a big gator like that. They have thick hides. But I didn't care. It was a release. And I needed one. A little kid, for God's sake.

"Shit, Jake! What the hell! That's a federal."

Sanchez knew my oddities, but this one surprised him. I was many things, but rarely impulsive. The two deputies in the dive unit looked at me as if I'd howled at the moon. One just shook his head. They knew what I felt. They had a shitty job too. Those poor bastards had to go down there in that murky water and retrieve the remains out of the truck. Human remains. The other gave me a thumbs up.

"Fuck it. They can bill me."

It became one of those reflective crossroads in life a man may encounter when he has an epiphany. The last one I had was after graduation, when I could have been a rock star with my garage band. I played a mean guitar, but somehow I found myself in law enforcement. Right after I dropped out of college. I ended up down in the Everglades. That was then. This was now.

The next day I turned in my badge. Retired from the CCSO—Collier County Sheriff's Office. Full benefits.

Two weeks later I left Naples and moved back up to my hometown of Clearwater. A week after that I became fast friends with George Dickel and Jack Daniel.

Two out of three ain't bad, I thought.

CHAPTER ONE

My name is Jesse Jake Randall and I'm a private eye. It says so on my office door. That office is in Clearwater, Florida, and that's my hometown. I look for things and people, and sometimes I get paid for it. I go by Jake. It's not short for Jacob, it's just Jake. I was in my office trying to reason with a hellacious hangover from last night. I hadn't made it home. Tequila, I think. My alligator boots were crossed at the ankles and were propped up on my desk. The blinds were drawn in an attempt to hold back the bright late-morning sun. The drumming in my head was accompanied by a light show on the inside of my eyelids. At least that's what I was watching. I dimly remember hearing the tinkling of the wind chimes I have on the office front door. It was either being opened, or my tinnitus was kicking in again.

The tall dame walked into my office and stood expectantly at the front of my desk. Really. Right at my desk. She had come in and marched all the way down the hall to my office. The receptionist must have been off that day. Anyway. Things were looking up. She was one of those high-profile, high-maintenance dames that only rich playboys and queer actors have. One eye focused on her and eyed her up and down. The other eye couldn't manage just yet. Black patent-leather high heels tied at the ankle. A light gray wool suit that clung to her curves better than Mario Andretti at Sebring. Blue silk plunge-neck blouse that showed enough of the Valley of Contentment that imagination could take the rest of the day off. Her amber hair was sun streaked, professionally coiffed, cut, and colored. Hazel-green eyes were clear and alert. High cheekbones, cute little ski-jump nose, and those lips. Full luscious lips in red's own red. I blinked and tried to focus, but she was still there. The light show wasn't going away. I tried to speak through dry cracked lips.

"Yes?"

"I need to hire you."

She said "need." Not "want to" or "I'd like to." Or even "may I." Used to getting her way. Not used to discussion. Oh, and a voice like tinkling crystal. I was sure I would wake up any minute.

I managed to ask.

"What about?"

It sounded like an old frog croaking.

"You need to stop a murder."

Pause. How do you stop a murder unless one's already being contemplated? Things got more interesting. The throbbing in my head reached a drumming crescendo as I forced Mr. Brain to go to work.

He wasn't very happy about it.

A fat white number 10 business envelope hit the desk with a noticeable thunk. I'd seen that movie before. A number 10 envelope always contained cash. Lots of cash. Crumpled, used bills. Filthy lucre.

Interesting just became curiously intriguing.

I looked up at her with the question in my eyes, and she explained.

"There's a ten thousand dollar retainer. There's more if you get the job done right."

Damn. Ten grand. One hundred hundreds. Ben Franklin, the centurion. That was essentially a quarter of this private eye's annual revenue. I decided this would be an excellent time not to mention that my standard retainer was a grand. And then only if I could get it.

The envelope got swiped into my desk's top drawer. There was life coming back. The drummer in my head was doing a solo.

"OK, let's hear it."

She glanced around. I nodded to one of the overstuffed chairs in front of my desk. She took a seat on the edge, knees together, those long legs crossed at the ankles, back straight, hands folded daintily in her lap. This dame had class and breeding. You could tell. It showed. What a dish.

"Well, I had a dream last night about getting killed."

Oh, boy. Mr. Brain was begging for the day off. My head was making throbbing sounds in my inner ear. It drowned out the tinnitus.

"A dream."

It was a statement more than a question.

"Yes."

I waited for her to continue.

She took a deep breath as she figured out where to start.

"It's about Bob Dylan's belt. He had auctioned it off for charity and I won the bid for it. It was a nice engraved leather belt with a large cowboy-style buckle. A *bas relief* of Bob Dylan in pewter. Maybe it was silver. I don't know."

Uh-oh, I thought. Mr. Brain was trying to wrap his arms around this. We'd never solved a bad dream before. Mostly insurance cases. Ten grand, I told him. Stay with it. It's ten grand.

I attempted a smile, and my chapped lips cracked and bled. She pretended not to notice.

"So it's time for him to autograph it. Dylan, I mean. Which will make it authentic and more valuable, I suppose. So I and my bodyguard spot him in the crowd and work our way over. But there's a rabid redheaded female fan hovering around him, and as I get close, she jumps up at me and stabs me in the neck. In the carotid artery. I see my bodyguard draw his .45 from his shoulder holster and shoot the woman in the head. But the knife is still my neck. Well, Bob Dylan's bodyguard sees all this, draws his pistol, and shoots my bodyguard. But he was only using a 9mm and my bodyguard had enough time to shoot both Dylan and his bodyguard dead before he died."

She paused and took a deep breath. She looked down, her impossibly long eyelashes fluttering. Reliving it was work for her. I wondered exactly how in hell I factored into all this. Mr. Brain was whispering in my ear. It came in over the tinnitus. Ten grand, Jake. Focus. Ten grand.

I paused and just looked at her expectantly, like I've seen psychologists do with their patients in those old movies. Waited for her to continue. It was a good play. I didn't know what the hell to say to her anyway.

At least she understood ballistics.

"So everybody's dead, and I've got to figure out how to get this knife out of my neck. I can't leave it in, but if I pull it out, I'll bleed to death in mere seconds. And on top of every-thing else, now I can't get Dylan's autograph on the belt. And I already paid for it!"

I could hear little capillaries in Mr. Brain popping and bleeding out. I was sure the blood was collecting in the whites of my eyes.

"What . . . I mean, what can I do?"

She looked at me as if I had farted at dinner.

"Do? You must stop that redhead from stabbing me!!"

"You said it was a dream."

"Yes. You need to find her and stop her from getting in it."

"I'm not sure I understand. Who is she? How'd she get in your dream? And are you going to dream a do-over, just so you can get Bob Dylan's autographed belt?"

A disbelieving stare.

"Well, of course."

I was not sure how to go forward. My liver was working overtime to process last night's tequila. My stomach was making noises even I had never heard before. And my tinnitus had my ears ringing like church bells.

Then my Zen kicked in. Solutions presented themselves. I knew exactly how to beat this. It was just too simple.

I looked at her for a long beat. What the hell. I had to go with it.

"I think I may have just the thing."

I rooted around in my bottom desk drawer where I keep all the stuff I don't need or can't use. There it was. A souvenir from the pub bar at the Harborview Club. It's the ritziest private club in Clearwater. Very exclusive. Top floor. Overlooks the bay. You know the type. Dark wood, lush ferns, expensive drinks, mediocre food. But a great view. I had saved it from that time I took Rebecca Lynn Russo there on a date. She was Miss Chamber of Commerce then and we were the social climbing couple to be seen with. But that's a story in of itself. For another time.

With all the pomp and circumstance I could muster, I presented the little pink drink umbrella to her. It had *Sword and Shield* printed on it with an image of a shield with a medieval heraldic crest and sword. That was the name of the place. The bar at the Harborview.

I hoped it would work.

"Go back to sleep and dream it all over again. This will protect you from the redhead, and you can get Bob Dylan's belt without any more trouble this time."

Her eyes glowed with almost childlike joy as she took the tiny umbrella.

"Wow."

I thought I heard the tinkling wind chimes again.

I had.

I looked up as a man appeared at the office door. He too had walked down the hall. Past the receptionist's desk. Following the voices, I guess. He was tall and very distinguished. Older. My age, maybe. European slender and impeccably dressed. Tailored Savile Row dark charcoal suit. Regimental tie. Windsor knot. Pocket square. Black wingtips.

I just stared. Mr. Brain was impressed. He spoke.

"Ah, there you are, love. It's time to go, I'm afraid."

He reached out his hand to her. She took it and smiled. I stood up. He didn't introduce himself.

"I do hope she was no trouble for you, sir." British accent. Plumy. Very aristocratic.

"Oh, no. Not a bit." I let my eyes feast upon her one last time. Maybe I'd see her again. Yeah, right, Jake.

"Right. Well. Shall we go then?" She stood, smiled, and slipped the little umbrella into her purse. That thousand-watt smile left me staring.

"Thanks ever so much."

I just nodded and tried to smile as they left.

The wind chimes on the front door verified their departure.

I plopped down in my chair and leaned back. Sighed. My alligator boots went back up on the desk. Mr. Brain wasn't bleeding as badly, and I desperately needed a drink. Anything but tequila.

Then it hit me.

No one had asked for the ten grand back. Ten grand, Jake. Did I really earn it? Don't go all altruistic on me, Bub. Yeah, we damn well earned it. The umbrella will work because she believes it will work. Mr. Brain had advised wisely.

Right. Moral debate over.

Ten grand.

I picked up my phone.

Dialed Rebecca Lynn's cell number.

Ten grand.

Rebecca Lynn, now my third wife, didn't take my call. Probably was with a client or in maybe court. In fact, she rarely took my calls. It used to piss me off, but then I learned to just ignore her rudeness. She's a prominent attorney, a legend in her own mind, and I'm just a normal guy who expects an answer to my very occasional calls.

OK. That's not fair. She's busy. Me, not so much. I cut her some slack. Hung up before the auto-answering menu chimed in.

Besides, the mood had passed.

I went downtown.

CHAPTER TWO

There's only one way to deal with a tequila hangover. Forget those old wives' tales. It's whisky. Real made-in-America sour mash Tennessee corn whisky. And in this whisky connoisseur's considered opinion, there are only two up to the task: George Dickel and Jack Daniel. You need not ask how I know. Your liver may hate you for it, but at least you'll feel better.

Mr. Brain was showing off. He wanted to contrast and compare the whiskies for me. Again. Both whiskies are sour mash, with a slightly different recipe, but Dickel mellows thorough an oak charcoal rick at ninety proof, and Daniel mellows through maple at eighty. Both are simply fine sippin' whiskies.

It was time to do battle with the nagging drum solo in my skull. The bar and pub was downtown, and during Clearwater Police Department's late afternoon shift change, it was frequented by PIs and off-duty cops, sheriffs, and other wannabe types who worked in the law enforcement field. And at the lunch hour, it was attorneys, judges, bailiffs and legal assistants who cluttered up the place. Drinks were always a good pour, and the food was fast. And good. And it was convenient to the Pinellas County Courthouse. And to my office.

I found a stool and slid onto it.

"Well. It's Jake Randall comin' in, then, init? You look like shite, laddie. Jealous husband kick your arse?"

That's what passes for a greeting at the Fort Harrison Pub in downtown Clearwater. It was a famous bar and pub, right on the corner at Fort Harrison Avenue and Court Street. It was currently owned by Gavin Connor MacFarlane, a Scot who lived in one of those fabulously expensive waterfront homes on Edgewater Drive on the way up to Dunedin. Everyone calls him Mac. Mr. Brain has no clue why. He thought Gavin— which means white hawk in Gaelic Scottish—was a suitable moniker. Anyway, Mac bought the Fort Harrison Pub years ago from a Turkish Muslim who had owned it forever and had eventually died. Before that it may have been a transplanted Cuban who originally owned the original frame shack back in the early 1900s. Like O'Keefe's down the street, it was part of Clearwater's history, like the Columbia Restaurant's bar across the bay in Ybor City was famous in Tampa; or Old Ebbitt's Grill in Washington, DC; or The Merger in San Antonio, Texas; or T. P. Crockmeir's in Mobile, Alabama. Or even Mozie's Saloon in Gruene, Texas, home to a hundred years of Texas cowboys. Or dozens of other famous centuries-old American watering holes with a long and vibrant history.

Fort Harrison Avenue was named for the actual US Army fort that was established in the early 1800s on Clearwater's high bluffs overlooking Clear Water Harbor. That's how the old maps of the area described the bay. Locals always called it Clearwater Bay. The fort was strategically located directly across the bay from a natural pass formed by Dan's Island— now known as Sand Key—and the south end of Clearwater Beach. Beyond that pass—Little Pass as it was called when I was kid growing up here—was the open Gulf of Mexico. Army cannons of the day could easily reach the pass and beyond. So the pass was well protected from any who may venture there. Anyway, nobody ever changed the basic name of the bar and pub. It had been a Clearwater landmark forever. The company was good, and the drinks were reasonable. You could even get good wings and a decent hot-pressed Cuban sandwich here too.

I replied to Mac's sardonic welcome.

"Nah. No such luck. Boy's night out is all. Me and Mark-boy."

"Aye, and you're looking the worst for it, me boy."

I nodded resignedly. Mac was short on diplomacy, long on factual observation. I guess I must have looked like I felt. I needed hydration. What I wanted was an ice water. What I got was a Jack and Seven-Up. My usual. Mac didn't even ask, just set it front of me. I nodded thanks, sipped my drink, and looked around. Mid-afternoon was always slow and the place looked it. Shift change for the police department wasn't for a couple hours yet, and the legal types were already back at work.

"Heard about the Boot Hill shootout you were in. Killed some nasty blokes from the Sandbox, I'm told. Now that's some good work there, init?"

Sandbox. So named to refer to the Middle East. Troops in Iraq came up with that. He was referring to an incident that occurred after my last case. That was about a week or so ago.

I was in a shootout with a couple of bad guys. Killed them both. My fifteen minutes of fame.

I didn't know then that that little gunfight would fuck up my life forever.

But it did.

It started out as a simple stakeout of an OSHA claimant. A normal run-of-the-mill case. My client is the insurance company. I was parked in the apartment complex where the claimant lives, watching his activities. Same old boring stake-out scenario. Sit in the car, drink coffee, watch the guy, pee in the jug. All night. Finally about midnight, the guy comes out of his apartment and goes to his car. I flick on my video camera. He opens the hood, checks the engine's dipstick, and begins to add oil. Now that's no big deal unless you're claiming to have been blinded in a workplace accident. My video camera on the dash clearly shows him opening the hood, checking the dipstick, reading the label on the oil container, and filling the engine. Not bad for a blind guy at midnight.

But behind him, way farther back in the parking lot, a very different movie was being shown. It caught my attention. Two guys were struggling with a bound and hooded young thing and were trying to shove her into a van. My bit for my insurance company client was done. I had the evidence of fraud on video. That was the extent of my job. I turn the video over to the corporate types, and they pay me. They can do with it as they please. Rarely does it go to court, but if it does and I'm called as a witness, I get paid a flat rate for that. So I didn't care. This one was a quick and easy job. And this job was done.

I was free to go home and go to bed. It was a compelling option.

But the abduction going on behind the fraudster had my undivided attention. Two physically fit males shoved the girl into the side of the van, and one perp got into the driver's side. Perp two was having trouble with the kicking and thrashing girl. I saw him punch her in the face a couple times. Shoved her into the van. Then he closed the van's slider and got into the cab on the shotgun side. The van roared off.

Well now. I'm an ex-cop, and to me that looked like a crime in progress. I put the Jeep in gear and slowly followed them out of the parking lot. They took their time, not speeding or doing anything rash, so I dropped way back. In the wee hours of the morning, it wasn't hard to keep them in sight. They drove around the residential areas aimlessly for a while and finally headed for the Clearwater Municipal Cemetery.

No good can come of that. Abducted girl. Midnight. Old cemetery. Not good.

That cemetery dates back to the very beginning of Clearwater, and it was nearly full. Had been for decades. It's what you'd think an old cemetery should be. A whole city block, with large oak trees, paved walkways, ancient marble and granite painstakingly carved headstones dating back a century and a half. A couple of huge ornate mausoleums. A perfect setting for a scary Halloween movie. Names on the headstones were founders and early movers and shakers in Clearwater. Some of my kin are buried there, and my family still had a plot. And unless you've got flowers for a grave or a prayer for friends or relatives residing therein, there's not a lot of good reasons to be there. Especially so in the wee early-morning hours.

I just hoped there wouldn't be a Halloween-style movie being shown here tonight.

I hoped wrong.

I killed the headlights on the Jeep when the van turned into the main cemetery driveway. Slowed down and crawled to the curb and watched. They were just about in the very center of the relatively small cemetery. The van had stopped next to an ancient grandfather oak. They thought it might provide some cover, I suspect. Perp two was pulling the still hooded and slightly more subdued young thing out of the van's cargo area. They were near an old mausoleum, and I could guess what they were up to. I left the Jeep on the street and stealthily headed in their general direction. There are no lights in the cemetery, and the street lights on its perimeter cast scant, faint illumination there in the interior. I made my way over to one of the oak trees, maybe twenty-five feet away from the side of the mausoleum. Perp one had pulled the girl's top off and had his pants down around his ankles. He was trying to flip her over. She was having none of it. They were clearly about to take turns on her. I watched for a moment to see how far they were going to go. Mr. Brain was deciding how to handle it. If it became a worst-case scenario. Then I heard them speaking a foreign language. It sounded like Arabic or Farsi maybe. I dunno. Guttural. Hard consonants. Just great. What the hell had I wandered into?

I carry a Kimber Ultra Carry chambered in .45 ACP. Always. As I watched the scene unfold before me, I pulled Mr. Kimber from my holster. Kept it pointed down with my arm straight along my right side. Finger off the trigger. Thumb on the safety. I stepped into the gravel driveway behind and slightly to the side of the van. Its engine was still hot and making little clinking noises as it cooled in the night air. My alligator boots made a crunching noise on the gravel alongside the paved drive as I walked up. Perp two saw me first and immediately pulled a pistol from his waistband and aimed it at me.

"Hey! Who the fuck are you? What you want?"

His English was passable, but noticeably accented. Even in the dim light, I could see him clearly. Definitely not a native son.

"Evening, gentlemen."

I nodded in the direction of the now topless girl.

"It's OK. Y'all go ahead. I'll go last. I'll just wait over here until it's my turn."

"What? Your turn? You get no turn! You got no business here. You get out of here."

His pistol came up higher. Face high. My face. Nine millimeter, I guessed. I'd had guns pointed at me before. Lots of times. But I don't intimidate easily. I scanned the scenario. Perp one was trying to get his schlong back in his pants and grappling to reach his own pistol.

Perp two was nervously glancing around. Looking at perp

one, then back at the girl, then back at me. The girl looked dazed. Out of it. She was pushed back on the steps of the mausoleum, her top still off. She didn't even try to cover herself up. Dazed. She looked to be of a lighter complexion than these two.

"Sorry, boys. I can't do that. I need you to put down your weapons. Raise your hands so I can see them, and step over here with me. Leave the girl alone."

Perp two was the excitable type. He was starting to jitter around erratically. Waving his pistol at me. Saying something unintelligible under his breath. Amateurs do that when they're rattled. And scared. I knew he would fire at me any second.

My arm came up with Mr. Kimber. I always carry in condition one, which means I'm cocked and locked with a round in the chamber. It's how you carry single-action autos.

My thumb clicked the slide safety off. It made an audible click. Perp one got his pants up and came up with his own pistol.

Pointed at me.

"Put your weapons down, and step away. Last chance."

"Who the fuck are you? What are you doing here?"

Perp one made that demand. And perp two had asked the same questions. Asked and answered. Amateurs.

Perp two fired first, but he was unfocused and the shot went wild. I hoped it hadn't hit anybody's house in the neighborhood. I went into a crouched Weaver stance and double tapped him center of mass. He dropped like a stone.

Perp one fired a half beat later, and he was wide. His second shot just grazed my left shoulder. I swiveled and fired at him. Two rounds of .45 ACP slammed into his open polo shirt, and he dropped.

The girl was wide-eyed and panting. Hyperventilating. The gunshots echoed in the still night air. Lights began to come on in the surrounding neighborhood.

I walked over with Mr. Kimber's sights still trained on the bodies that now lay on the ground. No one was moving. I kicked the guns away from dead hands. The girl's head was lolling, her eyes distant and unfocused. She seemed fine for the moment, just dazed. Probably drugged her. She barely knew what happened.

I holstered Mr. Kimber and picked up the blouse that lay next to her on the mausoleum steps. Draped it over her shoulders. She looked up at me uncomprehendingly but pulled the blouse around her.

"You're gonna be OK now. It's over. Help is on the way."

I dialed 911.

Dispatch answered on the second ring. I gave her the scenario.

"Shots fired. Casualties. Two shooters down and neutralized. Officer, uh, no, make that one good-guy civilian is armed but unhurt. One female abduction, possible rape victim. Incapacitated. Probably drugged. West driveway entrance, Clearwater Municipal Cemetery. Need ambulance and paramedics."

It was second nature for me to call 911 or backup in a shooting, but Mr. Brain had to remind me that I wasn't a police officer any more.

He was right.

I gave my name and phone number. Left the Jeep out on the street so it wouldn't be in the way.

Several minutes later it looked like a midnight parade on Myrtle Avenue. Blue and red and white lights everywhere. Clearwater PD and EMTs, Fire Rescue, several ambulances. And a couple reporters who had been monitoring the police radio frequencies.

Lights started to come on in neighboring houses. People

still in sleepwear were wandering out.

Exciting night.

A few minutes later I was giving Detective Ralph Hamilton, Clearwater PD, my story. We have known each other for years, and we've even solved a couple of cases together. He took my statement. It was pretty straightforward. I witnessed the abduction in the apartment building parking lot, followed them to the cemetery. Caught these morons literally with their pants down. About to have non-consensual carnal knowledge with the obviously unwilling female. They wanted to shoot me for interrupting them, but that didn't work out too well. There wasn't much in the way of conflict of fact. Several witnesses in the neighboring houses were already outside and were more than happy to give statements. They all verified my account.

Sometime later two gurneys, with dead bodies strapped to them, were rolled into back of ambulances. The girl was treated at the scene, then she too was on a gurney and loaded into an ambulance. But she'd go to the Morton Plant Hospital ER. The two perps were headed for the city morgue.

Then it was all over. The EMTs, fire rescue guys, and cops all finally drove away, leaving the neighborhood to gossip and recount the night's excitement. And then ultimately go back to bed.

The Clearwater Police Department got the collar, but I got recognition in the paper next morning. Above the fold. Local hero saves damsel in distress. Shoots two bad guys in a foiled rape attempt in a dark Clearwater cemetery. It was a story made for going viral, which it did. It was offbeat, kinky, and macabre all at the same time. The press did a fine job with that, too, and the tongue-in-check references to Wyatt Earp and the O.K. Corral were rampant. But I got in print with full photos and biography.

It was a boost for my business reputation. And to Mr.

Brain's esteem.

It didn't do jack for my bank account.

Mac had referred to it as the Shootout on Boot Hill. Gun fight in a graveyard. I get it. Very funny. The name stuck.

"Thanks, Mac. Lucky night, that's all." I sipped my drink.

"Luck is for old ladies and young lads, me boy-o. Men need to be ever watchful. You watch yourself or you'll get that tight arse of yours shot off one fine day."

"Never happen. I'll die quietly in bed."

"Aye. And probably with some fair lass who's not yours."

I just grunted and shook my head. Never verbally spar with a died-in-the-wool Scotsman. You'll just look outclassed, and it annoys the Scot.

The whisky was doing its job. I was feeling a little better. Mr. Brain seemed like he was starting to function again.

The drummer in my head was on brushes now.

But the tinnitus hadn't let up much.

I eyed the pub's décor again. The Scottish flag, blue with the white cross of St. Andrew, hanging over the bar. Mac's own MacFarlane clan tartan made up the backdrop for the very rare and expensive bottles of Scotch whisky stored in the ancient glass-front oak cabinet. It brought a little old-world charm to a very new-world Clearwater.

There was a reason.

Mac lived in Dunedin, just up the road on Ft. Harrison Avenue from the pub. It's almost a Clearwater suburb. The name comes from *Dùn Èideann*, the Scottish Gaelic name for Edinburgh, Scotland's capital. And Mac's home town. So naturally his pub ended up being Scottish themed. That was just perfectly fine by me.

All was becoming right with the world. I was ready to head home. I figured I would have one more drink, then stop on the way home and pick up some takeout for dinner.

Chinese BBQ ribs and some wings. Pork fried rice. I could live on that. Maybe an avocado salad and some salsa and Melba toast for her.

We could eat light at home.

Open a nice wine.

Maybe just catch a movie on TV.

Lounge back. Nice and easy.

I just hoped Rebecca Lynn would be willing to be there too.

CHAPTER THREE

My office condominium contains four offices. There's a file room, a bathroom, and a conference area too. Mine was the big window office in the back, and I used the conference room and the file room for my business. Once in a while. I rented out two other one-room offices as a full-service professional executive suites operation. The income helped with all the attendant expenses associated with owning a professional office condo. Lots of expenses. Association dues. Insurance. Taxes. Upkeep. Wi-Fi.

My private investigative work was mostly investigating personal injury insurance fraud cases, and they all paid scale. It was a minor scale too. You really couldn't live on it. So I rented the suites. It was a little better than breakeven, but it was working for me. Besides, it added some much needed human activity to the office. At least when there was more than just me here.

I was tired of doing office clerical stuff. I was restless. I decided I'd done enough for the good of the cause for today. I left.

I went to the houseboat.

I used to live on the houseboat. It was relatively small and perfect for a reclusive, grumpy in-between-Mrs. Randalls-bachelor like me. The slip rent was cheap. And it included shore power. But that was before I moved in with Rebecca Lynn. She's an up- and-coming litigation attorney. She was pretty good at it. Her arguments got written up occasionally in legal review publications. I'd read them, and they would always impress me. She had a great legal mind. But litigation attorneys can be vicious. Brutal. They can gut you like a fish. While they smile at you as you just watch your guts spill out. It's unnerving. Everybody wants to be on her good side. Including me. Of course, it didn't hurt that she was once Miss Chamber of Commerce either. That was years ago. She still had it. Beauty and brains and success. It's a deadly combination for a guy. We dated a bit, and the chemistry was definitely there. We fucked like muskrats for a couple years. Anywhere and everywhere.

She'd drag me around to all of those attorney bar and chamber of commerce functions, and I know her crowd pretty well. They knew me. We were certainly an odd couple. She was upwardly mobile. I'm less so. I'd chat up the attorneys and judges and social climbers that frequented these things. It was always fun. They're basically focused on themselves, and I'm kinda philosophical about all that. Besides, once in a while I'd get a referral from one of them. But I always sent my soon-to-be-guilty clients to Rebecca Lynn. They knew I would. How could I not? She'd have to send some of my referrals out to others—conflict of interest, you know—and these attorneys always knew where that client came from. It was a symbiotic relationship, I guess. That's why I'd even go. To these events, I mean. There were usually some hors d'oeuvres served. That meant neatly dressed wait staff meandering around carrying silver trays of beautifully crafted little morsels. Smiling. Free. I'd always take one. At least I'd get something to eat. Rebecca

Lynn would have a wine and some crackers and cheese. I'd have a Jack-and-Seven and go hunt for shrimp or those bacon-wrapped scallops. Wine and cheese for her. Seafood and whisky for me. Described us perfectly.

Even though she's twenty-some odd years younger than me, she had me move in with her. It was her demand. Who was I to say no? I quit trying to analyze the psychology years ago. I like slender younger women, and she's probably got some latent daddy issues. Electra and Oedipus complexes merging. I get it. So what. We're both brainy. We like to play chess with each other. I never let her win. She wins only occasionally. We discuss eclectic things like metaphysics and the meaning of life. Zen in all its forms. Dharma and karma. The relationship was working for the most part. Mostly. It was a resume enhancement for me. Everyone thinks I'm some kind of well-hung stud. Well, I am that. For her, I dunno. Maybe the same but in a different way.

Anyway, I keep the houseboat for times like this when I need to be away from the world for a while. So I clambered aboard and opened the slider aft of the cabin. It was dark and dank down below as boats typically are. I opened it up to air out. The smell of gasoline, salt air, and bilge was familiar and welcoming. Except when I was hungover. It was time to hunker down a bit and just mellow out. I popped a couple Ester-C tabs. Vitamin C in mega doses always works for me. Plopped down on the bunk and closed my eyes.

But I couldn't shake the mysterious dame encounter. Bob Dylan's belt? How do you solve a bad dream? What the hell was that all about? Was the dame loony? Why didn't Messr. Astor ask for the money back? That's what I called him. Did he even know about it?

I felt kinda guilty about taking the money. For about twenty seconds. The envelope was still in my desk drawer. I solved the case, right? Obligation satisfied. But I just couldn't make it work. Too many bizarre angles.

And somehow I felt that it would come back to haunt me. Easy money always does.

I needed a nap and, thankfully, I finally dozed off.

* * *

I awoke somewhat refreshed, and my work ethic kicked in. Either that, or Mr. Brain was nagging me to go back to work. He was usually right, so I got up and got dressed.

And headed for the office. Again.

One of the individual suites in my office condo was occupied by a mental health therapist. Marie Vaughn had a master's degree in psychology and specialized in tutoring learning-challenged children. She was an ageless beauty who had it all: brains and style and class. She and I would spend hours comparing the merits and shortfalls of my psi functioning to her psychological analysis. Especially as it pertained to criminal motivation and mental makeup. Very heady stuff. Her eyes would twinkle in a certain way whenever she thought she had me in a philosophical debate. And I definitely noticed her eyes. She was intellectually stimulating, and I admired and respected her a great deal. We would debate issues, all in fun, and I guess she felt the same about me. Her husband, Ted, was a retired real estate investor who was chronically ill. Cancer or something. I had done some things for him in the past, and I introduced him to Mark-boy as a real estate connection. I always got the impression that there wasn't much between Ted and Marie, but I never pursued it. You know—don't ask, don't tell. I could relate. Rebecca Lynn and I were in the same boat. Actually, Marie and I never delved into our relationships with our spouses. Not in any depth anyway. Not for any particular reason, really, other than personal discretion.

But Marie and I enjoyed challenging each other intellectually. We always seemed to be on the same page on most issues. But there was a noticeable current—a vibe, maybe—that ran through some of those discussions, and I know she was aware of it too. If Rebecca Lynn wasn't in my life, well, let's just say Marie would be.

I stepped out into the hall. I wanted to tell her about the dame with the Dylan bad dream. Just to see what she could make of it. But she had her Do Not Disturb sign on her closed office door. That meant she was in session. She was busy. Damn. I went back into my office. Picking Marie's brains would have to wait.

Another office suite I rented out was to a couple of college dropout types who were into all things computer. Twenty-somethings aspiring to be the next digital tech gods. Not focused on it though. Smart guys, I guess, but intellectually all over the map. Spent most of their time searching the web and its deeper underbelly for conspiracies. The deep web, the dark web, whatever that is. They'd uncover some arcane bit of lore and then charge into my office breathlessly enlightening me about the Bilderberg Group, George Soros' Nazi past, Area 51 sightings, alien moon bases, UFO encounters, or the bugs on Mars. Whatever. It was fun to watch that youthful exuberance. God knows mine was on the wane. They were partners in their company, an LLC I helped them create, and they did research for me sometimes. They were pretty good at finding stuff online. And sometimes they couldn't quite make the rent. So it kinda worked out in a barter-based sort of way.

David Willis was a tall, lanky guy, and oh so serious. Wound pretty tight. Wore his hair early Johnny Depp. Everything had to have meaning, a purpose, and one had to be aware of this to get ahead and find enlightenment in life. He was opinionated and cocksure of everything. All the time. It was amusing for a while, then it got old. But you couldn't ignore him all the time. Sometimes he was right.

John Cavanaugh, his partner, was a polar opposite. He was stocky, but not fat, and had a gentle humor and intellect about him. He had those sensitive eyes that chicks dig, was soft spoken and wore his hair business cropped. He was an artist type, in perfect contrast to David's hyper and analytical persona. He had his art displayed in local coffee houses and in an occasional professional office. It was very good; he was a realist. His landscapes looked like photographs, they were so real. And he could do dinosaurs so well that some textbooks commissioned his artwork. But he didn't draw or paint. He created them pixel by pixel on the computer. Digital art, I think it's called. He'd sell a landscape occasionally for good money. It would piss David off no end. He hated to be upstaged. Together they were pretty adept at what they did. It's just they really didn't do it much. Intellectually spastic nerds. Living at home. Or in the office.

I was in my office reviewing an insurance case. I was figuring my time. Had to see how much money I lost. Six hours on surveillance should have paid me a per diem plus expenses. The insurance company only would pay an hourly. Take it or leave it. They didn't care. For that reason—and others—this would be my last job for them. Watching some guy mow his lawn or hump his wife when he's claiming to be disabled from a minor auto crash was not only mind numbing, it was beneath me. I had pride. But I did it anyway.

The phone rang. I checked the caller ID. It was Russell Davidson, the liaison from one of my insurance company clients. His job was to interact with us private eyes. Keep us interested in accepting his claims cases. My primary contact. Picked up the phone.

"Jake Randall."

That's how I answer the landline.

"Jake. Russell Davidson here."

Davidson was no charmer. All collegiate arrogance and thinly veiled disdain for guys like me who actually work for a living.

"Hey, Davidson. To what do I owe this honor?"

No mister. No first name. Last name familiarity for him. I know he hates it when I call him that. That's why I do it.

"Hey, I saw your write-up in the paper last week, Wyatt. Very impressive. You're now a famous guy. But tell me: have you shot anybody lately?"

Did he just call me Wyatt? This shootout shtick was starting to chafe. He snickered into the line. I chortled along. That's okay. Tit for tat, I guess.

"Ah. That's a good one. No, I've already killed everybody around here who needs killin'."

"I see. Well, Jake, all this cowboy shootin' aside, I called because I wanted you be aware of how insurance fraud is such a significantly huge hit to the economy. According to FBI stats, the insurance industry—collectively consisting of some seven thousand companies like ours, as you probably already know—will lose some forty billion dollars or more a year through payment of fraudulent claims. Forty billion, Jake. Think about that. That's a huge hit to America's economy"

Oh, God. It was one of those oh-so-personalized, pump-up-the-energy calls. I'd get one every couple of months or so. Just to remind us lowly PIs that we're doing God's work in investigating and exposing insurance fraud. Saving the American economy. Worse, I knew he was reading it off his computer screen. I gave him a noncommittal response. I knew I'd have to endure yet more.

"Uh huh."

He continued.

"While it's true that the insurance industry as a whole takes in more than seven trillion dollars in premiums each year, you're aware that some of that money goes back to our policyholders in order to make whole those who have suffered a regrettable and tragic loss. It's how we protect our customers from life's inherent risks. It's what they've asked us to do. And what's left over after we pay those claims, Jake, is invested back into the American economy in such rock-solid ventures as annuities, residential housing, and commercial real estate."

More infomercial. I hated these calls. I hated insurance companies. But they paid the bills. Some of the bills anyway.

I pondered the dust and dirt on my alligator boots. Buffed them on my pants leg. Davidson wasn't done yet. He had to get to the flag waving rah-rah close.

"So our hats are off to guys like you, Jake, who enable us to keep our policy premiums as low as possible by weeding out those illegal and fraudulent claims. And for that, we thank you!"

A comment from me was expected at this point in the spiel. His computer screen probably displayed "wait for comment." I obliged.

"Well, that's awfully nice of you to say, Russ."

Davidson also hated it when I called him Russ. Like during these intimate moments we share over on the phone listening to these mandatory infomercials. So that's why I did it.

But I wasn't quite done yet, either.

"And, Russ, I can't tell you how much that means to a small private investigator like me. But in all fairness, you know, if insurance companies weren't so interested in making obscene profit on top of obscene profit, like funding annuities and housing and commercial real estate projects at confiscatory interest rates, perhaps those poor aggrieved policyholders of yours would not have such high premiums. Or those huge fucking deductibles."

There was a pause on the other end of the line. There probably wasn't an appropriate prompt on his screen for a comeback like that. Which means he'd have to wing it.

"Uh, Jake. We're all on the same team here. No need to get sarcastic."

"Oh, that wasn't sarcasm, Russ. That was a heartfelt observation."

I loved tweaking him. I'm an ardent red-blooded capitalist, and I appreciate insurance companies being the source of capital for many a commercial project. But I loved keeping him off balance. For the two-hundred grand a year salary he was pulling in, he could put up with a little rebellious snarkiness from one of us lowly PIs.

Davidson decided to wrap it up.

"Well, nevertheless, Jake, I—err, we—appreciate your efforts in getting fraud reduced. And I'm looking forward to continuing to work with you. As always. And keep that six-gun loaded, partner. Yee-haw and take care."

"You too, Russ."

Fucking idiot.

I was primarily focused on the personal injury aspect of insurance fraud, but I still had to endure these infomercials periodically. And nothing would happen to me because of my little verbal rebellion. They needed me, and I just needed to get it off my chest. All that infomercial public relations bullshit notwithstanding, insurance companies hire guys like me to find a reason they don't have to make good on their policy. I get paid so they don't have to pay your claim. And don't kid yourself. You're never fully insured. Not really. I always felt I needed a shower after an insurance case. Goddamn vultures.

David Willis saved me from letting myself get seriously

pissed off. He came blasting into my office and, in one fluid motion, slid into one of the overstuffed chairs. Threw a leg over the arm and stared at me. I was supposed to be curious. I was just miffed at the interruption. And still working on getting myself pissed off at the cheap-ass, greedy insurance company infomercial.

"Guess what."

David loved to start conversations that way. It annoyed me.

"Bucs won?" The Tampa Bay Buccaneers were having a decent season, but I just said that to irritate him. Following sports was beneath him.

"What? No, I dunno. Guess again."

Sigh. I looked up. Time to give it up and play along. After fifteen minutes of Russell Davidson's nauseating and insultingly patronizing spiel, I wasn't in a very good mood anyway.

"OK. What?"

"Somebody just shot Bob Dylan."

He could have said that an asteroid was going to hit Earth in ten minutes. Or that the San Andreas Fault had ruptured and California had slid into the Pacific. It could not have hit me any harder. I just looked at him, mouth agape. Mr. Brain was trying to wrap his arms around what David was telling me. I could only stare at him for what seemed like minutes. Finally I managed to speak.

"What? Dylan? Whaddaya mean?"

"Jake, dude, wake up. Somebody shot Bob Dylan."

To anyone else that would have been just another celebrity news oddity. Click bait. Dylan's shot. Or Mick Jagger's latest wife had another baby. Or Lady Gaga performed with her clothes on. Or Rosie O'Donnell uttered something intelligent. Or Michael Moore is on a Jenny Craig diet. Big yawn. But to me it was catastrophic. Illusion had just become reality. And it wasn't even my illusion.

"Who? I mean, how do you know?"

He just gave me one of those condescending looks. How does he know anything? I already knew. This was serious. I just couldn't believe it. Precognition? Psychic functioning? How could . . . I realized I didn't even know her name. The dish. The hot dame with the bad dream. And that gentleman. Didn't get his name either. How could she or he or they know about Dylan getting shot? From a dream? I was sold on that dream-story case. In, out, and paid. Case closed. Was it merely a coincidence? I didn't believe in coincidence. I resisted the urge to check the desk drawer for a large white number 10 business envelope. But this was beginning to seriously spook me.

I must have looked pale.

"You all right? You're pale. What, were you, like, a Dylan fan?"

I just stared at him. Mr. Brain was doing calculations. No time for idle chatter.

"Jake?"

David laughed nervously. He looked concerned. I was rarely without a witty and acerbic response. This was one of those times. He asked again.

"What's the matter with you?"

Was it news? Rumor? I had to confirm the veracity of this astounding news. I tried it again.

"How do you know this?"

"Wow, man. It was just an alert on the newswires. There was a video too. It just happened. They don't know if he's OK or dead. Why are you so freaked?"

Why, indeed.

I wondered if I should tell him. I wondered if it even happened at all. The dame and her dream, I mean. I was in a sorry state when I learned of Dylan's demise. Maybe it was all just a hallucination. Mine. Or maybe the dame's. Or for that matter, maybe this second Dylan shooting didn't happen either.

Mr. Brain needed some time to work out what the hell was going on.

"Newsfeed, you say? Can you forward that to me?" I didn't want to waste time with an internet search that would give me everything about Dylan except this.

"Sure. Stand by." David unfolded himself out of the chair and headed back down the hall to his office.

I opened the desk drawer. The worst feeling came over me when I saw the envelope. That part of the bizarre scenario was true, it seemed. Gently opened it. Hundreds. Crisp. OK, now I knew the dream dame incident actually happened. The rest I'd have to sort out. Something told me to keep the money on the down low. I don't know why. Instinct, maybe. One thing that was still bugging me was why I was paid so much. Ten times my normal retainer. To solve a bad dream? And in cash? And literally in the first thirty seconds of the meeting? Was it tainted money? Blue dye from a bank robbery job? Counterfeit? I'd wait until the office was deserted, then I'd check. Sequential serial numbers? I hoped so. I could at least track that part of the source. Or maybe not. Cash transactions over five grand are tracked by the feds. Naturally I didn't have a source at . . . wait. What government agency is it that does that anyway? Tracks deposits? I'd have to find out. I bet this money didn't go through a bank. Nowhere near a bank. That was the one thing about this crazy deal that I was absolutely sure of.

The envelope went back in the drawer. The drawer closed. I looked up.

David was back. Stuck his head in the door.

"Yahoo News. Google it."

I nodded.

Just great. That was the last thing I was going to do. I didn't have time to sort through a search, knowing the returns would be everything in the world about Dylan except this. And I sure as hell didn't want any more of the Bob Dylan's belt mystery. Too fucking weird. Somebody would most likely come for the money. They'd want it back. Maybe.

Mr. Brain was working on the cosmic meaning of this surreal deal. He thought it was just a series of events that seemed to have causation. But what cause? Maybe it was a catalyst for something else. But with serious cosmic overtones. Or worse, maybe it was karma emanating from dharma. The universe reminding me who was boss. Who was really in control. Testing me with a philosophical puzzle.

I was just a peripheral player in the universe's random number generator. Dealing with the reality of things. Deism as observed by a modal realist. And I didn't want any part of this weighty and confounding mystery. But it had happened. I was there; now it's done. Move on. Next. But sometimes you get events in life that are unfathomable. Things that make you wonder about inevitability. Fate. Predetermination. Hand of God. Things like that. This was one of those times.

Anyway, what I wanted was for it to just go quietly away. What I got was a screaming monkey climbing on my back. Gnawing on my skull.

Damn.

I was majoring in philosophy when I dropped out of college late in '68. I ran out of money for school, and I got drafted as well. The Viet Nam conflict was beginning to get really hot, and me and a lot of guys my age were invited to go on an overseas tour. Courtesy of Uncle Sam's draft. But the US Armed Forces couldn't use a guy with a chronic medical condition. No matter how gung-ho he may be. So I got a 4-F classification. Unfit for duty. Damn. It was both a relief and an insult at the same time.

Then I heard something in there. A clatter. A bump? A grunt?

With my shoulder against the door jamb, I rolled silently into my office, following Mr. Kimber as I quickly scanned the empty room. Clear.

Years ago, when I bought my office condo, I had a small and discrete exterior door cut into the back wall of my office. It opens outside to the lush quadrangle. Then I built a little patio out of paver blocks directly outside. Had a deck chair and a small table out there too. I use it only rarely, like when I step outside to get some sun or some fresh air or to smoke a cigar.

Tonight it was standing open. Wide open. And I was looking through the back door opening at the common area's landscaped and sculptured lawn in the quadrangle behind my office condo.

I stepped over and through the door. Looked outside. The quadrangle is well lighted at night. No prowler.

But my chair was knocked over onto its side

I swiveled around, looking for disruption in my office. Filing cabinets, computer, desktop. All seemed to be in order. Check. I closed and relocked the back door. Stepped over to the desk and pulled open the drawer.

The envelope with the one hundred hundred-dollar bills was still there. I nodded a curt hello to Ben. Closed the drawer.

Mr. Brain figured we came back too soon and spooked the spook.

Whoever was here got away. Clean.

Just then I heard the roar of the big American V-8 engine as the Suburban blasted out of the parking lot.

I sprinted back up the hall and bounded through the front door. Ran out onto the walk. Put the Kimber's sights on the speeding SUV as it ripped by me. The Suburban fishtailed as it squealed out of the parking lot driveway and onto the street. The driver had the pedal to the metal.

It happened too fast to take a righteous shot. And beyond the target and across the street were other offices. The possibility of a stray round causing collateral damage was high. And I didn't have reasonable cause to shoot anyway.

Worse, I couldn't make out the tag.

Exasperated, I holstered Mr. Kimber.

Mr. Brain shrugged. Home team zip, visitors one.

Peachy. We lost. We had nothing.

I went back in.

Double-checked all the doors and locks.

Office was secure.

It was late. I was tired and pissed off.

So I headed back to the houseboat.

For the second time.

* * *

Some Yankee asshole motored his boat through the harbor pulling a heavy wake. Moored yachts rolled and pitched. My houseboat rocked and slammed against the pilings. Stuff creaked and clinked inside the cabin. Woke me up. There's a no-wake zone in and around the marina, but there's always some dickless fool who can't wait to plane off. He probably rented it. It's always a Yankee transplant, because real locals understand the effect of wakes on moored boats. They have respect. Yankees don't. Or don't care. Pinellas County Sheriff's Department has a marine division, and they get to write tickets for excessive wakes. And nautical stupidity. There's a lot of stupidity going on in Clearwater Bay. So they write lots of tickets. Liveaboards like me have no sense of humor when it comes to boat wakes.

I needed to get up anyway. What I wanted to do was to use the time to meditate. Use my metaphysical yoga training to attain an alpha brain wave state. That's an altered and calm state of mind. Self-imposed. Reveals insight. It allows me to see things clearly. Used this method for years when I was with Collier County Sheriff's Office. Solved cases that way. I was younger then. I had to work harder at it now. I needed clarity right now. What I got was to lose my concentration and fall asleep. It happens occasionally. It did this time.

I was up. I didn't get to the alpha state I wanted. Didn't get any insight into my present conundrum. And I never got my drink. I was busy straightening up the disruption caused by the dickless Yankee boater's wake.

Then Mark Forrester came by.

"Permission to board."

Mark-boy and I go way back. That's what I call him. Don't really know why. Just one of those things that grows legs and sticks. We grew up in the same neighborhood, went all through school together, did all kinds of guy stuff. Inseparable. Raced cars. Rebuilt Porsche engines, raced them. Raced boats. Skied all day. Raised hell. Shot guns. Sailed the Gulf and some of the Caribbean. Imported some contraband. Screwed a lot of dames, smoked a lot of weed, hiked a lot of mountains. Amazing, we never got arrested for any of it. Or killed doing it.

"Come ahead."

Mark-boy stepped into the cabin and looked around. Then looked at me disapprovingly.

"When you gonna clean this rat's nest up?"

I just shot him a look. He likes to fuck with me. I'm ship shape and squared away at all times. Despite dickless Yankee boaters.

"So. What are you up to?"

I asked that, ignoring his barb. Mark-boy was a member of the idle not-so-rich. His time was his own. He was a builder and a real estate broker, but he only did any work when he was cash shy. Or felt like it.

"Huntin' you down. Figured you'd be here in your sanctuary."

"That I am. What's up?"

He looked around the cabin expectantly.

"Where's my drink?"

That was Mark-boy. He'd been aboard about ninety seconds before he hit me up for a drink. After he ragged me about the boat. He liked to show off. Drank his whisky neat. But only when he was showing off. Like that time we were at that early 1800s historic cowboy bar in Gruene, Texas. Mozie's Saloon. He was knocking them back like there was no tomorrow. In Gruene, there wasn't.

I poured a one-ounce shot for each of us.

"Next time you come by, bring a bottle."

I slid one of the shot glasses towards him. He knew I usually drank mine with Seven-Up. Today I had a shot glass. It was that kind of day.

"You're not gonna put mixer on that? No Coke or nothin'?"

Mark-boy can sometimes play that raggin'-your-ass scene a little too effectively. I wasn't in a good mood anyway, and this was one of those times.

"You gonna drink, or are you just gonna stand there and annoy me?"

Mark-boy grinned and raised his glass. At least he knew when to shut the fuck up.

"Cheers."

We tossed back the shots.

"So. What brings you out here to my yacht?"

"Ah. Glad you brought that up. Several things."

He waited for a response. He didn't get one.

"First, for a free drink. You are such an accommodating host, cap'n."

His raised his now empty glass as a salute. I cracked up. Not mocking, not patronizing. It was so over the top. He could always break my bad moods. That was Mark-boy. I poured another shot.

"And?"

"And second, to recruit your sorry ass for a sailing adventure. We're going to take the *Perihelion* out for a couple of days. Or maybe longer."

"Well, now. You have my full attention."

The *Perihelion* was a Cheoy Lee designed and built ketch. God's own sailboat. Some years ago Mark-boy sold a couple of high-end apartment complexes and made enough in commission fees to live off for the rest of his life. Or so it seemed at the time. Being an avid sailor with saltwater in his veins, he flew halfway around the world to Hong Kong. There he bought a handmade Cheoy Lee. A 1970s vintage mahogany-clad Offshore 41 ketch. Only about eighty of these magnificent sailboats were ever built. Probably fewer than half of those are still in service. And he had one. The deal was the Cheoy Lee people would sail it across the Pacific as far as the Panama Canal. Mark-boy had to take delivery there. In Panama. Then the stupid son of a gun sailed that beast solo across the Gulf of Mexico all the way to Clearwater. Ballsiest thing I ever saw. After that, we sailed it all over the Gulf. Usually with the lee rail under. With its clean lines and high aspect ratio, it's fast, luxurious, and beautiful.

That got my interest. Big time. But duty called.

"I'm working on a case."

"A case? No way. No, Jake. We're hitting the high seas. I won't take no for an answer. We sail down the coast to Ft.

Myers, and maybe cut through the ditch—"

The ditch. He was referring to the Caloosahatchee River. It cuts across Florida from the Gulf to Lake Okeechobee. Then there's a canal that connects Okeechobee to the Atlantic.

"—then head out for Bimini. Nah, the ditch is too slow, too shallow. We'll just shoot the Straights, go up with the Gulfstream to the Bahamas, and just get lost . . ."

I just looked at him while he played out the fantasy, as I deciphered the meaning. Recruit me means he needs me for crew. And to help buy stores. Which I was more than glad to do. Motel and gas money was unneeded with the wind and salt spray in your face. And a heaving deck beneath your feet. But days could become weeks. Weeks could become months. The Bahamas may be a destination, but we could end up anywhere. Such were adventures with me and Mark-boy.

Basically there was no plan. Just an urge.

And he wanted to leave tomorrow.

It was an invitation I wanted to accept. Badly.

But I couldn't. Not tomorrow. I couldn't ignore this gnawing Dylan bad dream thing. It was screwing with my head.

Besides, Rebecca Lynn had a couple events "planned to attend" for this week. That pretty much meant that *I* had a couple events planned to attend for this week. That was okay for the most part, I guess. You put on a suit, go to the club or some ritzy upscale hotel conference room, get a drink, and meander around the room making small talk with the movers and shakers who invariably frequented these things. During these events I'd be picking the brains of judges and lawyers. It was usually boring for the most part. Sometimes, though, a decent conversation can happen. I avoid politics and religion. I keep my comments confined to legal matters and judicial concepts. When in Rome, do as the Romans do, you know, that kind of thing. Most lawyers are either anal retentive and can only talk about their fields of practice, or complete space cadets who can only deal in lofty theoretical legal issues. Especially judges. But I had some questions about the civil and criminal legalities of dream manifestations and hoped I would be in the company of fresh brains to pick.

And I hadn't been able to chat with Marie Vaughn to find anything at all about psychological side of the implications of the manifestations of bad dreams. Could there be a legal concept if one were to act on events in a dream? Especially as *mens rea* applied to un-enacted-upon crimes to be. The intent that comes before the act. Pre-crime.

That seemed pretty theoretical. I wasn't aware of any case law arising from something like that.

That's why I wanted to qualify it.

Mr. Brain was becoming suspicious that our loony dame may be setting me up for something. And I wasn't sure, either. Maybe by having prior knowledge of an attempt to commit murder. But on whom? Kill Bob Dylan, for crying out loud? It made exactly no sense.

But I couldn't shake the possibility.

She seemed kinda squirrely, after all.

In spite of her beauty.

So I'd take this opportunity to explore the legal side. Work those lawyers and judges a little bit.

Earn my money.

And there might be bacon-wrapped scallops there.

CHAPTER FOUR

Every hundred-dollar bill tells a story. You wouldn't believe the arcane information that's contained on a single bill. The Bureau of Printing and Engraving started using a whole new design on bills years ago beginning with the Series 1985. And then changed it again five years later. To make it harder to counterfeit. That was the goal anyway. Newer bills, from Series 1990 and beyond, have a security strip either printed onto or woven into each bill. Those changes went on other denominations of bills too. But aside from that, you can tell where the bill was printed and what Federal Reserve region it was sent to. And other arcane bits of information. Just by reading the bill. If you know how to read the code that's printed on them. But once it's been in circulation, it's just cash. Tracking is almost impossible.

I finally got the courage to analyze my newly gained wealth. I chose a time when no one else was in the office. I don't know why. Maybe my training kicking in. Or paranoia.

I spread the bills out on my desk. All of them. So far not good. Very interesting. All the bills were the old style and design.

The hair on the back of my neck stood up. I looked carefully at a couple more randomly selected. Held them up to the light. Then each in turn. I rooted around in a desk drawer till I found my magnifying glass. Studied each bill, front and back. They were all old-style, pre-security strip bills. Series 1985 with the small Ben Franklin portrait centered on the obverse. Still valid, but old, and some of this series were still in circulation. But getting more and more rare as time went on. Bills get old, so they're recalled, destroyed, and periodically replaced by Treasury with new bills. And they were not sequential serial numbers. Random bills. Mr. Brain was doing calculations. My stomach was growling. Palms began to sweat. These were all pre-security strip bills. Series 1985.

All of them.

Damn! All of these are older style bills. Very old. Thirty-some odd years old. It's statistically unlikely for them to be of a uniform series in a tranche of ten thousand dollars. Especially if they're drawn randomly from the general circulation. Worse, they didn't look like they were that old. They weren't crisp, but not in the crumpled, worn, and torn state one might expect. These had to come from someone's safe. Or some archive or the like. Or they were counterfeit. I looked at them, all laid out neatly on my desk. They were consistent in their quality. I could not find any flaws, any ink smears, or any blending or bleeding of the microprinting. But still, to get one hundred old-style bills randomly chosen from the general currency from circulation? It wasn't likely. So if I've got a hundred of them, all the same series and all the same quality, they must be counterfeit.

Lovely.

Well, now. Quite possibly I was in the possession of counterfeit, bogus money. Supernotes. Those are counterfeit bills so perfectly made that they are virtually indistinguishable from real legal tender. Illegal. Fake money. Worthless. I'd read about supernotes some time ago, but it was just as a passing novelty regarding counterfeiting. I wasn't an expert on the subject. Now it looked as though it could be possible—hell, very likely—that I had a bunch of them. Counterfeit bills. Normally when counterfeiters pass worthless notes, they do it in a tranche along with real money. Maybe on a one-to-five ratio. Real mixed in with fake. But these all seemed to have the same quality printing and fabric. All were real. Or all were fake. I really couldn't tell for sure.

What the hell was going on? Mr. Brain ran down the chronology. It didn't look good. A client with a bad dream. Excessive payment. No names. Maybe fake money. And why did they come to me? What kind of scam was being run here? And worse, who would pay a detective an outrageous fee like this? With probably bogus bills? It made no sense. Was I being set up? Maybe. For what? It sure didn't add up.

I sat down. Stared at the possibly worthless paper on my desk. Part of me was disappointed in that I wasn't ten thousand dollars richer. Like I was five minutes ago. Part of me was intrigued. Part of me was paranoid that I was possibly involved in a felony. Possession of—and dealing in—counterfeit money. Great. Just what I needed. More chaos in my life.

Easy money. You want it, but there's always a downside. I needed to be sure the bills were bogus. That meant trusting my bank. And that meant possible exposure.

To what I didn't know. Great.

I did what I had to do.

I called Nick.

Nick Hollister was my main contact at my bank. I'd known him for years. He was the branch manager at the branch I always used. I wanted to keep this off book, so I didn't want to go inside. Inside the bank, I mean. If I met with him in the bank and the money was found to be counterfeit, he'd be duty bound to confiscate it. And me. I didn't want to put him in a situation like that. Or me. So I sent him a text. Told him I'd buy him a drink after work.

He was happy to take me up on it.

I was settled in the back booth at the Fort Harrison Pub when Nick walked in. Nick is the typical banker. Young, late forties maybe, very sharp, and completely wrapped up in all things banking. He was always willing to enlighten me on esoteric banking issues. He certainly knew his subject. Money. Currency. Leverage. Cash flows. I guess it was exciting for him. He was a banker after all.

He looked around, spotted me. Waved and came over.

"Hey, Jake. What are you up to now?"

If I offer to buy drinks, Nick knew I'd be picking his brains. Last time we chatted, it was about structuring a currency exchange. French francs exchanged for dollars one weekday morning, then back into francs that evening at close of business. Take the yield—the money—and run. It worked out pretty well. So he didn't mind a bit.

When the drinks and a small order of wings and nachos hit the table, I took a pull on my drink. Nick was focused on the nachos. I leaned forward and dropped the bomb.

"Tell me everything you know about counterfeiting."

Nick paused, looked up at me strangely, and let out a low whistle.

"Oh boy. That's a pretty broad topic. What aspect?"

"Let's just say I find an envelope in the back of a cab. And in that envelope I find a few hundred-dollar bills. Series 1985. How can I tell if they're fake?"

Nick flinched when I mentioned Series 1985. He knew that denotes the year of that bill's design. That told him I had said bills. He knew they were old style. Thirty-plus years old. Back in circulation. And pre-security strip. And he probably knew I couldn't determine if they were, in fact, legal tender.

"Eighty-fives? Really? You got it on you? Can I see it?"

"Off book? Just you and me? Down low?"

He gave me a look.

"Of course."

I palmed the bill under one of those cardboard drink coasters bars always have scattered all over. Slid it over to him.

Nick swiped the coaster into his lap, and retrieved the bill. He scrutinized it for a couple minutes. Snapped it. Fingered the fabric. Rubbed it between his fingers. Held it up to the light to see through it. Discretely.

"Well, I hate to tell you, I can't tell. If it's fake, it's a good one. Supernote, probably. Can you tell me anything more about it?

"Nope. Found it and a bunch of others in a cab."

Nick just looked at me. He snorted and laughed cynically. He knows I don't ride in cabs.

"How many do you have?"

"Ten grand worth."

"Jesus Christ!"

Yeah, that was my prayer too. I was no further to the truth on this. I asked him if I could just deposit the money. And not go to jail.

Nick snorted again.

"I wouldn't necessarily go that route. Convert them would be better. Exchange for like value. Or you could use one of those chemical pens."

Nick paused and looked at me.

"Or you could just turn them over to the FBI."

This time I just snorted. Ignored that suggestion.

"A couple of the bills had black pen marks on them, so somebody tested at least a few. Tell me about supernotes."

Nick sighed. Leaned back, still fingering the bill in his

hand. Took a pull on his drink. I guess it was starting to worry him too.

"Well, as you know the early bills—like the Series 1985 you have here—didn't have a security strip at all. A lot easier to counterfeit. But after the 1990 series and beyond, Treasury started a microprinting technique. They printed a quasi-visible ribbon in the bill. It was just a thin strip in the bill that read USA100 over and over. But that series still used the small portrait of Ben Franklin. In the center of the obverse side. Subsequent series were primarily the same. Treasury didn't start the embedded strip until just a few years ago. Series 2003, I think. Used a different portrait, actually a much larger Ben Franklin portrait, too, and it was offset left of center. It had much, much finer microprinting that you can't see without a magnifying glass. Or a loupe. All these changes, of course, were implemented to thwart counterfeiters."

Nick grabbed a nacho, paused thoughtfully.

"That was the plan, I mean. Or at least make it harder to duplicate accurately. The security-strip bills have been in circulation for years, as you know, and in the early days, spawned all kinds of conspiracy theories. Some people believed the strip was a magnetic tracking device that could trace the bill's migration through the M1."

He looked up to see if I knew the jargon. I did.

"The M1 is the measure of the actual currency in circulation."

I nodded impatiently. I remember the craziness that followed the introduction of the security strip.

"On the early series, the strip was just printed on the bill. Not woven. As I said, it too just reads USA100 over and over. It's just hard to reproduce that effect if you're counterfeiting. But the later series had the strip actually embedded. Woven into the bill itself. That essentially stopped counterfeiting by photocopy. But it drove conspiracy theorists crazy. They thought there was a magnetic chip or something imbedded in that strip that would track the bill—and also the user—no matter where it was."

Nick laughed at that.

"No such luck, I'm afraid. They have GPS satellites to track everyone nowadays. There's no need to worry about being tracked by money."

Nick paused and laughed again at his cynical comment. Hell, he was right, Mr. Brain thought.

He took a sip of his drink.

"But it did make counterfeiters work harder and make better bills. Hence the rise of supernotes. And supernotes in the earlier bill series. Like 1985s."

I interjected.

"Yeah, I read up on that, but this whole idea of supernotes left me kinda skeptical. Way too James Bond-ish."

Nick laughed.

"Yeah, I know. But it's true. In the last twenty years or so, several bad actors have popped up and are suspected of counterfeiting bills so perfect they are indistinguishable from real ones. To me, that would indicate some rogue element in a nation state—that is, a government—was printing them, just by virtue of the fact they're essentially identical to real ones. These bills are so perfect they are beyond the capabilities of any individual mom and pop counterfeiters. The days of using a copier to make funny money, I'm proud to say, are over."

He continued.

"But North Korea was one country accused of distributing supernotes some years ago. The US put pressure on them to cease and desist alleged—"

Nick did finger air quotes at alleged.

"—said distribution. In fact, the US had already investigated three Asian banks for that very reason and actually pro-hibited Americans from banking with those banks. Seriously. Prohibited Americans from using those banks. Just because of suspicions of them printing and distributing fakes. The Treasury Department takes counterfeiting pretty seriously, as you can imagine. Naturally, these banks collectively disputed the allegations and said the only time they had knowingly handled counterfeit money was in 1994 when they discov-ered ten thousand dollars in counterfeit hundred-dollar bills. Note they said "knowingly." They subsequently did turn over the suspect US hundred-dollar bills to the local authorities. Under heavy diplomatic pressure, I might add. But we, that is, the US, threatened them—that's North Korea I'm talking about—with sanctions over their alleged involvement with these supernotes."

"Alleged."

Finger quotes again.

Right. Always alleged. Clearly Nick was being diplomatic. I was very worried that the amounts and timing of all this seemed to coincide with my ill-gotten wealth. All that hap-pened back in the mid-1990s, but it looked like the same thing was happening all over again. Everything old is new again. It was looking more and more like they were in fact counterfeit. But counterfeited by whom? And how did they come to me? And more to the point, why? Lovely.

Even clearer was somebody wanted some free money. They probably printed a lot of it. And there was still a lot of that bogus cash loose in the wild. In fact some of it was in almost assuredly in my possession.

Betsy came over and stood expectantly by the table. She was waiting on us today. I looked up, momentarily distracted from Nick's in-depth lecture on counterfeiting. She's about thirtyish, kinda cute, and always seems to wait on me at the

Pub. Sometimes she and Mac double team me, raggin' my ass over something or other. It's to be expected when you're a regular, I guess. All in fun. Like family. Hell, I ate it up.

"Another round?"

Nick shook his head. I didn't.

"Comin' right up."

Then she paused, turned back around, and looked at me.

"Hey, Jake. Dave says you may be sitting in with them tonight. Is that right?"

David Albright was another lifelong friend from the old neighborhood. Semi-professional musician like me. His band, Studio Boys, was playing tonight at Haughty Jelly's. They were the defacto house band there, and people loved them. They were good, too. Tight. Rock and roll all the way. Another rhythm guitar is always a plus for a four- or five-piece rock band. Ask Lynyrd Skynyrd. And I played rhythm.

"He mentioned it, yeah. I will if I can."

She lit up. Flashed me a smile.

"Neat. Well, I hope you do, because I'll be there. They asked me to help out on the bar after I get off work here. I love seeing Dave and all you old guys still trying to rock out. It's so cute."

"Oh. Well. Thanks, I guess."

She flashed another big smile, and laughing at her little dig, dashed off. Nick just sat through the exchange and finally totally cracked up. In spite of the interruption.

"You've got quite a fan club going, Jake. Here you are. A famous detective. Killer of bad guys. Rock-and-roll star. Damn, who knew?"

I just looked at him and grinned. He was still laughing at the incongruity of it all. I shook my head resignedly. What can you say to an exchange like that anyway?

It reminded me of a story.

"That reminds me of a story."

Nick just looked at me oddly. Like I was stealing his thunder by going off on this tangent. Or maybe he thought my attention had waned.

He was right, it probably had.

But I went on anyway.

"The first time my band played before a really large crowd—a thousand people maybe—was way back at the Clearwater Bayfront Auditorium. It was just a modified old Quonset hut right on the bayfront here in Clearwater, and the city used it for concerts, dog shows, art expos, Star Spectaculars . . . you know, whatever. My band was competing in the Battle of Bands, and Dave was in the audience that night taking photos of all of us on stage. We all knew each other, of course, so we all shared in the glory of each other's short-lived local fame. Anyway, me and John, our lead guitarist, came on together at stage left. The drummer, bassist, and keyboardist came on from stage right. Very cool and dramatic. And on the first chords of the first song, my high E-string broke. Just popped at the bridge and hung down off my guitar—you could plainly see it. I was devastated. Had no chance to change it, we were already on. So there I am, in the spotlight, for the rest of our gig, trying to play on five strings, with my E-string gone."

Nick just looked at me as if he had just heard the biggest non sequitur in the world. Maybe he had.

I decided not to elaborate any further. Betsy had already heard it anyway.

I shrugged. My dad always said you should remember your experiences in life, if for no other reason than when you're old and sitting in your rocking chair on the front porch, you'll have some stories to tell.

Well, I just told one.

Nick cleared his throat, pulled on his right ear, and tried to get back on track.

"Ok, where was I? Oh, yeah, the history of counterfeiting."

Nick was just warming up. His knowledge base on banking topics was vast and untapped. I took another pull on my drink and noticed that Betsy was still grinning at me from behind the bar across the room. She stuck out her tongue at me. I gave her the finger. She broke up laughing. Nick grabbed a chicken wing. I perked up, ready to learn.

Nick continued.

"Well, it gets worse. Same year, in 2005, five Brits were convicted in the UK for printing up US hundreds. They cranked out three and a half million bucks all within eighteen months. And in 2008, the CIA itself was accused of printing funny money to fund some of their off-book foreign ops. One expert I read claimed that the bills were so perfect that only a government agency could have made them. The CIA! Can you fathom that? No one really knows what happened to any of that cash. The FBI hasn't collected anywhere near those amounts in busts, I can tell you. As far as I know anyway. So you got all kinds of bad actors screwing up the economy with worthless currency."

Mr. Brain was collating this new information.

"So you're saying that if these bills are counterfeit, they're so well done that even hardcore experts can't tell the difference? Can't tell if they're real?"

"Pretty much. And the CIA certainly does have that kind of access through the Treasury Department. It's not only plausible but *probable* that the CIA could have been cranking out bogus paper. I mean, if you had the right equipment and the plates and the inks and the fabric, you can make money."

Nick snickered at his pun and tossed his second wing bone back on the plate.

Mr. Brain wasn't amused.

"But, Jake. Look at it this way. If these bills are printed by the UK or North Korea, the government has a case to make that they're counterfeit. And they would be, of course. So in that case you'd be in deep doo-doo by holding counterfeit paper."

"But if the US did it, even through the CIA or some other part of the shadow government—

Nick paused. Looked around again. Leaned forward and, in a conspiratorial tone, continued.

"—how can it be said that it's counterfeit? If they're using Treasury equipment—exactly the same plates, the same inks, the same fabric, and same everything? How is it counterfeit? It's still backed by the US government in that case. Only the guys who actually printed them would be able to tell for sure. And maybe even they can't tell the difference once the bills are in the wild. You know, in circulation. In the M1."

In the wild. Yeah, I knew about the wild. There were one hundred of them in my desk drawer.

Mr. Brain was thinking about getting richer. Nick paused again.

"So in the latter scenario, yeah, I'd say you're golden. I would avoid depositing it in a bank, however. In an abundance of caution. You know, just to be sure."

Right. Just to be sure. Spend it freely, Jake. Just don't go anywhere near a bank with that shit. Mr. Brain was busy searching for precious metals distributors. Funny money for silver, maybe. I hit pause. Mr. Brain stopped searching. We'll just sit on the dough for a while. It may come in handy when—not if—I get my hands on this Dylan dreaming dame.

Nick glanced around. Started to slide the bill back over to me. I made an executive decision. Shook my head.

"Keep it. A souvenir. Frame it, hang it on the wall. For morbid curiosity, if nothing else."

Nick looked at me. Then down at the bill. I could see him

weighing the same issues I'd been struggling with for the last several days. Finally he looked up at me and smiled. I knew I was safe.

"Thanks, Jake. I will."

I still had ninety-nine hundred left, and Nick's information was so good, I couldn't complain. Even with drinks and wings factored in, it was a good meeting. I felt a hell of lot better. I had plausible deniability in the event of an extreme worst-case situation. Like if I was holding phony paper. But even if the dough was bogus, it was OK. It was so good it was good.

Mr. Brain was happy. We were still rich. But he still wanted silver. Or even maybe gold.

I just hoped Nick didn't come to expect gratuity like this in the future.

After he left, happy with his net gain, I texted Rebecca Lynn. I was relieved and happy. I texted her phone. I wanted to take her to dinner. Meet somewhere. Just the two of us, catching up. Quasi-romantic. Couple of drinks, maybe even something more. By the time she returned my text, I needed another drink.

I looked at my phone's screen as her replies scrolled by. Read the bad news:

"Sorry. No can do."

"Ate early and am in a meeting."

"Will be here for a while. Be home late."

"Don't wait up."

Looks like I'd be eating alone or not at all.

I ordered the drink.

Lately we were close if we were in the same area code.

It was getting old.

CHAPTER FIVE

Rebecca Lynn rolls out of bed around 5:45 a.m. Oh-dark-thirty. Career gals need extended time in the morning to get ready. There's hair and makeup and wardrobe that need attention. Live with a woman and you know. I'm a light sleeper, and when she's up, I'm up. It's not a choice, it's just I'm awake. While she occupies the bathroom, I go downstairs and make coffee, get the paper, and feed the fish. Mornings consist of little conversation. It takes a while for Mr. Brain to get with the day's program. Same way with her too. She works her crossword puzzle to stimulate her analytical side. I read news portals on my tablet. Not much in the way of conversation. Unfortunately. Sometimes, maybe we'll trade dreams. That's always revealing. To me anyway.

Her interest in me seems to have waned. She may have another male interest, I dunno. I'm a PI, but I'm not gonna investigate my own wife. No way. Truth will come to light--if that is the case—when it's ready. I guess I just didn't really want to know. I'm in my late mid-sixties, and I've retired several times in my life. Successfully. But I always got bored and had to go back and do something. Un-retire. Like now. A private investigative consultant. Not really full time. I only take cases when I feel like it. Rebecca Lynn's my third marriage. I'm her second. Both our ex's remarried. We used to joke about it. I'm in good shape and can do whatever I could do in my twenties. Just can't do it as long. Rebecca Lynn is in her mid-forties and I'm sure she's sublimating. That's all. Our sex is both rare and perfunctory. All her energies go into her career. At least I hope that's it. It's not like there's another man, really. It's more like there's no man in her life at all. It scares me sometimes. She's at her peak in earning potential, and she's good at her career. Famous attorney. She has social aspirations as well. Board member of this, chairman of that. I don't want to be a drag on that. I'm not a social climber. It's boring to me. So I basically leave it alone. I think she knows how I feel, but she either doesn't care or doesn't want to contemplate my reasoning. She's focused on her. I have quite a bit more unscheduled time in my life to fill than she does.

I'd just like to fill some of it with her.

"I thought we might have lunch one day this week. Whaddaya think?"

I was fishing, but I hadn't been with Rebecca Lynn for more than twenty minutes at a time in a coon's age. I wanted some me and her time together.

"Aw, honey. I can't. I'm back to back for the next week or more. Evenings too. I have two new clients, and I have to do the initial intake on them. Big cases. Sorry."

I was sorry too. It sounded a lot like last night. I played the chivalry card.

"No problem. I know you're slammed."

She shot me a quick smile. Turned back to her crossword. I returned the smile and took a pull on my coffee.

"Maybe we can go somewhere for a weekend getaway next month."

"Sounds good."

Verbal dismissal. No commitment. No enthusiasm. Certainly no follow-up. It hurt. I went back to reading my news sites.

I remembered the first time I met her. It was not long after I had retired from Collier County Sheriff's Office and moved back up to Clearwater. It was the first day of the third month of what I hoped would be another great year. She walked into my office. Really. Walked past the reception area, down the long carpeted hall, and right into my office. Bold. I was sitting at my desk. On the phone. Doing business. She took a seat. Looked around the office. She got up and studied my wall plaques. I wrapped up my conversation. Hung up. Eyed her. Slender, decent figure . . . willowy, with long blond hair. She had on some kind of flowery dress with black knee- high leather boots. A jacket of some kind. Odd way to dress down here south of the South. They dress like that up North. When she spoke I knew right away she was from Chicago or thereabouts. It was that unmistakable nasally adenoid accent. Introduced by some mutual attorney friend.

Her spiel was all self-promotion, grandiose and uninteresting. Mostly bullshit. A typical Yankee carpetbagger, I thought. Still, I gave her forty minutes of my time as a courtesy. We chatted a while about nothing and everything. Just wanted to meet me; networking, she explained. Fine. Meeting over, I walked her out to the hallway. Watched as she sashayed back down the hall, past the receptionist's desk, and out of my office condo.

I was picking up multiple vibes from her. Deep inside her was a vulnerable, frightened woman-child. That appealed to me. Brought home my paternal instincts. That protect-the-women instinct all men have. But wrapped around that was a shield of arrogance, narcissism, and inflated and misplaced self-worth. She hid behind that. Not so appealing. She was an enigma, to be sure.

I walked back into my office, shaking my head. I must have known even then that she would completely and totally fuck up my life. She was bad news for me. *Don't fuck her*, Mr. Brain advised wisely. Whatever comes of this, for God's sake, just don't fuck her.

Four months later I fucked her.

That was several years ago. Now we're a married couple that rarely sees each other. A few shared interests. We're close if we're in the same zip code.

I think we love each other. I know I'm in.

But couples get like this when the spark goes out.

Damn shame.

Mr. Brain reminded me that nature abhors a vacuum. And my social calendar at the moment was vacuous. With Rebecca Lynn's immediate sans-Jake schedule firmly etched into my memory and she on her way to work, I dialed Mark-boy. I wanted to see if he had left yet. On his spur-of-the-moment sailing adventure.

He picked up on the second ring.

I opened, straight to the point.

"Still in town?"

"For now. Might not be leaving at all. I dunno."

"Why? What happened?

"Oh you know. Stuff."

Stuff. That could mean anything. Money crunch. A woman. Maybe he even found a real estate listing and had to actually go to work for a couple months. Anyway, the Grand Bahamas adventure was on hold. Indefinitely.

It was apparent the cosmos was trying to get my attention. This could only mean one thing. I should go to work. Rebecca Lynn's working. Mark-boy's probably working. Marie's working. No one can come out and play. Shit.

I headed for the office.

I was still concerned about the breaking and entering episode the other night. Who would want to break into my office? For what? And why? I do lame-ass insurance fraud cases. Mostly. Boring, mindless, and certainly not sexy stuff. For the cash? Maybe, but who would know even about that? Kids, maybe? On a lark? Not likely with an expensive government-issued looking Suburban in the mix. If you took randomness out of the equation, you got a planned and definite act.

Somebody wanted something I had. Or knew.

I put Mr. Brain on the case. I had other more mundane chores to do.

It was quiet. None of my tenants were in, so I had the place to myself. I decided to do some mundane clerical chores and get caught up on things I'd been putting off. Mail. Email. Phone and text messages. I really hated tasks like those. It seemed to be going in reverse, responding to things that already happened. Looking at the past. Playing defense. Not for me. I like offense. I like forward momentum, like anticipating the next move.

The phone rang. I keep a landline, I guess, just for some sense of tradition. It rarely rings, except for unsolicited sales or unwelcome stuff like that. Like the annoying Russell Davidson. And if it rings and the caller ID is unknown, I just let it ring. If it's a valid call, they'll leave a message. Everyone uses a cell nowadays. Hell, I use the same procedure on my cell too. It's accepted standard operating procedure.

I recognized the caller ID immediately and picked up the phone.

"Frank, you lazy Cuban half-breed! How the hell are you?"

It was Frank Sanchez, my ex-partner from back in my Collier Country Sheriff days. I hadn't talked to him in a while.

It was good to hear his voice.

"Jake, you old broke-down, half-assed crazy bastard. Are you even still alive?"

Guys who are good friends talk to each other like that. It's just a guy thing. Guys don't get mushy and feely, we get rough and crude. It's comforting. And it works for us. We chatted on for a while. He told me about his new blue-water fishing boat. I couldn't top that, so I didn't say anything. That was OK. I hoped he had won the lottery. Most detectives can't afford a boat like that, even if he got it through an asset forfeiture auction. He didn't elaborate. I didn't press it. Private investigative consultants don't make the steady income with benefits that county sheriff detectives do, even in sleepy Collier County, so he loved ragging my ass about buying power. His, not mine. He knew I always wanted to learn to fly and buy a cheap Piper or a Cessna, but never got around to it. It was nice of him to remind me. My bucket list wasn't getting any shorter. And there wasn't a single strike-through on it. So it was a lopsided game of one-upmanship. He won. Finally he got to the point of his call.

"I got a missing persons case up your way. You still do those?"

Still do those? Hell, they were usually more boring and messed up than insurance cases and, as such, took a heavy toll on one's psyche. So sure, I still did those.

Self-torture was my bread and butter.

"Whaddaya got?"

"Meet me in Sarasota and I'll go over it with you."

Well, now. Things just ratcheted up several orders of magnitude on my holy-shit-what-the-fuck meter. I paused. He knew that would get me. This was becoming interesting. I immediately went into security mode.

"Sensitive?"

"Very."

"What level?"

"Sarasota, Jake. Yes or no?"

He had me and he knew it. If this case was so sensitive that Frank Sanchez needed to play it on the down low, it meant it was black. Deep black. Damn, I thought. The end of boredom just rang me up out of the clear blue sky.

"OK. Send me a postcard."

That was spook-speak for a low-tech communiqué. He would send me written instructions as to where to meet and when. Landlines weren't secure. VoIP phone lines weren't secure. Email wasn't secure. But old-fashioned letters sent through the mail were relatively secure, especially if you re-used an old envelope that was innocuous. Like with a return address from a well-known source. My favorite was IRS. No one, and I mean *no one*, would tamper with or intercept an IRS notice.

"Done. Look for it tomorrow. And Jake? Keep your head on a swivel."

"Roger that. Duly noted. And you watch your back."

We rang off and I sat down, leaned back, and propped my alligator boots up on my desk. I couldn't help but run through some scenarios. A missing person case so sensitive that we had to meet on neutral ground to exchange information? That was intriguing enough right there. But what really worried me was the concern I heard in Frank's voice. He's a lawman's lawman. Never saw him rattled. Not like the laid-back, deep-thinking Christian-Buddhist-Pantheist philosopher I am. Always looking for the hidden meaning. Not Frank. Frank was a just-the-facts-ma'am kind of guy. He was either scared or worried, and that alone was enough to scare the shit out of me. Despite my growing concern, there was no way I could have turned him down.

What I wanted was some blue-water sailing time. What I got was some serious back-to-reality. But what's the worst that could happen?

Mr. Brain reminded me that bad choices make good stories.

I pulled my Kimber .45 from my hip holster. It hadn't cleared the holster since the shootout in the cemetery. Time to clean and lubricate it. I dropped the magazine, checked the chamber, and re-holstered. Snagged my range bag on the way out. Headed to the range. I needed some serious trigger time first.

The range I go to is pretty upscale. Great lanes, well ventilated and lighted, good target retrieval system, and it's indoor and air conditioned. I paid for a lane and put on my ear protection. Went through the double doors and set up on the firing line. I hadn't done any shooting since the cemetery thing. I ran through a couple of boxes of ammo. My target had a two-inch hole just slightly to the left of center of the main body mass. Nine o'clock on the x-ring. After I punched out the hole, I was merely throwing lead into that empty space. My skills were honed already; now I was just wasting ammo. As I pulled down my last target and cleared my weapon, I turned from the firing line.

A crowd of folks had gathered behind me watching me shoot. They were grinning, and a couple nodded to me. One guy gave me a thumbs up. They knew who I was. And about the shootout. Probably read about it in the paper. They just wanted to watch me shoot, I guess. It was high praise from a tough crowd. I know I shoot well; it's a skill I've always had. But I still felt a little embarrassment at having been the center of attention. Then again, it felt pretty damn good.

Even some of the guys at the Fort Harrison Pub picked up on Mac's comment and had started calling it the Shootout at Boot Hill. Very clever. They would buy me an occasional drink, though. Out of admiration and respect. I appreciated that: their acknowledgement meant something to me.

OK . . . a *lot* to me.

As to the two worthless pieces of shit that I killed that night, I didn't give a good goddamn about them.

They weren't the first.

They won't be the last.

CHAPTER SIX

Two days later I was on I-75 headed towards Sarasota. It's only ninety minutes or so from my office in Clearwater, so I didn't need to remain overnight. Just drive down and back. Which meant I didn't have to tell Rebecca Lynn. Or anyone else. She wouldn't have probably cared anyway. It was a day trip, down and back. For Frank, though, Sarasota was considerably farther away for him. He'd have to come up from Naples. I wondered why he didn't split the difference. Meet halfway. In Port Charlotte, maybe. It must be he wanted to be farther from Collier County. Or maybe he just wanted to drive all day, up and back.

The letter came in the mail the day after I spoke with Frank. It was a bill from Geico. I don't have a policy with Geico, so I knew it was from Frank.

Ringling Museum of Art 13:00 mañana was handwritten in red ink on the invoice. Nothing else. I guess he wanted to be sure I noticed it. I did.

Ten minutes later I was in the Jeep. Headed south.

I was sitting in one of the Ringling Museum's galleries studying a four-hundred-year-old Peter Paul Rubens oil on canvas. It was huge. A little over fourteen feet high and about the same width. Floor to ceiling. *Defenders of the Eucharist* was the title. Rich vibrant colors, incredibly fine minute brush detail. A couple of plump pink cherubs. Typically Flemish religious painting of the 1600s. Masterful.

Frank sat down on the cushioned bench next to me. I hadn't heard him come in. But I wasn't startled. Mr. Brain was lost in the grandeur of the seventeenth-century depiction of God's encompassing love that was looking down at me from the gallery wall.

"How the hell did they paint those huge paintings hundreds of years ago? How did they keep their perspective on a canvas that damn big?"

It was a valid question. I often wondered that myself. I wasn't that good with crayons, so something like this old masterpiece was a mystical marvel. Peter Paul Rubens. Amazing skill.

Frank looked around the huge, empty room. Then continued.

"CCSO got a BOLO from the FBI three days ago. Missing woman. Last seen in Clearwater in the last few days. She's integral to certain FBI investigations of foreign actors counterfeiting US currency, international money laundering. Works for Secret Service. Goes by several aliases."

He palmed a USB flash drive into my hand. Continued to view the paintings.

"That's the file on her."

"If she's been spotted in Clearwater, why did they send the be-on-the-lookout to y'all way down in Naples?"

He paused and looked at me. I could see the questions and concern in his eyes.

"Jake, it was sent to you at Collier. That's why I called you."

"What? Why did they send it to me? Counterfeiting and money laundering aren't technically my specialties. And not only that, but you're telling me the FBI doesn't know I'm no longer a deputy down there? After all this time? That's hard to believe."

"Maybe they know more than you're giving them credit for. What the hell have you been doing in the last few years to get their attention?"

Indeed. What had I been doing? Surveilling insurance frauds. Killing bad guys. Chasing funny money. Christ. I looked at the flash drive in my hand. Mr. Brain was screaming for time out. Too much information too quickly. Money laundering? That hit pretty close to home. Missing person? Wait a minute. Could this missing dame be the same loony one with no name with a bad dream and probably counterfeit hundreds? The one who dreams of Bob Dylan's belt? And she's possibly a missing Secret Service agent? How much more bizarre is this case going to get? What the hell was happening here?

Panic was pounding on my door. Mr. Brain was hiding under the bed. He just wanted a drink. Frank was looking at me in his detective mode. My armpits were wet.

"Holy shit, Frank. What in the world is going on?"

"I hope you know, my friend. If you don't, you better get a handle on this thing right the fuck now, because it can and will eat your lunch in a hurry."

I stared at the flash drive. Then at the magnificent paintings hanging on the museum wall. Religious paintings depicting how God loves and protects us all. I sure hoped so. I expected to wake up from this surreal bad dream any second. But I knew better. I was in a nightmare that wasn't a dream. Like Bob Dylan's belt. What in God's name had I stumbled into?

I shoved the flash drive into my pocket.

"Frank, I don't know what the hell is going on, but I can tell you I had a situation a couple weeks ago. And I need some time to sort it all out."

Frank paused for a beat. Looked at me hard.

"A situation."

I briefly told him about the hot classy dame and her bad dream she wanted me to solve. And how she paid in cash. Lots of cash. Her aristocratic escort. And that I had initially thought it was just a case of some rich dame acting out her delusions. And that I had put it aside as a case closed. And then I told him about the shootout on Boot Hill that happened a few weeks before she entered my life. And finally about the break-in at my office after all that. Those three events happening so close together were just too coincidental. But how, I could not yet see a connection. If there even was one. All the while I was unconsciously feeling the flash drive in my pocket. I pulled it out again.

"Christ, Jake."

It was way past time for prayer.

"Yeah. Tell me about it."

I paused. Mr. Brain needed to get on the ball. To help me out. I dragged him out from under the bed. He was squealing.

What I wanted was answers. What I got was more questions. But I needed questions. The right questions. I looked at the flash drive in my hand.

"Who else knows about this?"

Frank just looked at me with incredulity.

"You mean other than the FBI and half the goddamn intelligence community?"

"Yeah. That's who I mean."

"Just you and me, in that case."

I exhaled a low breath. This will take some deep meditation, I thought. I'm in the middle of something I know nothing about. I didn't like that one bit. I looked back at Frank.

"Buy you lunch?"

There is a fabulous high-end café on the Ringling campus. They serve artfully styled and magnificently crafted morsels, extravagantly priced. You could still get a good old American burger there, though. And they have a full bar.

And I needed a drink. Mr. Brain was lobbying hard.

Frank shook his head. He stood up, stretched and glanced around. We were the only ones in that immense room.

"No, I'm gonna head on back down. I'm on the clock. Thanks anyway, though."

He stopped and turned around.

"Look. I know this is a strange situation, to say the least, but if you need any help from me on this end, just let me know."

Frank was like that. He was a good man, a good detective, and a good friend. I just nodded. What can you say to that anyway?

"I just might. Thanks."

Ten minutes later we were both back on the road. Traveling in opposite directions. Back to our own lives.

Frank's information weighed on my mind all during the drive back to the office. Nothing made any sense. I struggled to see a pattern. Dame with a bad dream pays me an obscene sum to solve her dilemma. The cash payment may or may not be counterfeit. FBI is looking for her. Or maybe not. Could be a ruse. They contact me. I couldn't see a connection. How did I figure in all of this?

When I got back to the office, there was nobody around. I made a cup of coffee. Looked at my desk and the clutter that covered the beautiful oak top. Stacks of mail and God knows what. I decided to do some housekeeping before I studied the flash drive. That always helps. Refocusing on a mundane chore tends to clear the mind for more intense analytical exercise later. Some may call that distraction. Or procrastination. I saw it as applied Zen.

And it gets my desk cleared.

I have two file drawers in my tall legal-sized file cabinet allocated for company paperwork. One is marked "Bills Payable." The other says "Past Due." Over time items generally passed from the former to the latter. It's not that I don't pay my bills; it's just that I'm not that good at it. It's a chore that's just too clerical, too procedural for my free-thinking mind. At least that's what I tell myself. Sometimes I could convince Marie to stop by and write the checks for me and post the books up to date. I really liked her company, and she would always lift my mood. She's bright and cheerful and amazingly competent. And she could just breeze through the task. I hated to impose on her, but it was easy for her, and she loved to do it for me. So it kind of worked out. I got the bills paid and paid Marie with the absolution of my guilt. She thought it was charming, and she'd always just laugh it off.

But she's been either busy or out for a week or so. Bills would have to wait.

So today the unsorted stack of papers on my desk went into one of those two drawers. The stuff that didn't match either category went into the round file. And that was filling up pretty fast. It was good therapy. Didn't get me any closer to answers, though.

I finally found the desk's top. It was an old surplus World War II army major's desk I'd had forever. Belonged to my dad. Which he bought from government surplus right after the war when he got home from the Pacific Theater. And it was old even then. Beautiful solid oak. Sturdy. Solid. I'd had it refinished some years ago. It was simple in design and GI functional. And it was most assuredly way older than me. I loved it for that reason alone.

But I couldn't find a reason to stall any longer. Couldn't put off the inevitable.

I plugged Frank's flash drive into my laptop. Normal intelligence agency file. Dossier. Opened the PDF files. Attached to the inner folder leaf was a photo. A picture of the dossier's subject.

And my heart stopped.

When I saw who it was, I had to remember to breathe. Mr. Brain shorted out. Went comatose. My what-the-fuck meter was pegged in the red again. It had been doing that a lot lately.

Staring at me with those hazel green eyes and those luscious red lips and thousand-watt smile was the dame who waltzed into my office with the Dylan bad-dream story. Same one who started all this. I recognized her immediately. How could I not? She's drop-dead gorgeous. Her real name is Margaret (Maggie) St. John, special agent, United States Secret Service. Holy shit. She really is a Secret Service agent. I thumbed the screen through the pages. Highly decorated. Rave reviews from her superiors. Commendations up the ass. File was thick with them. Ran undercover ops all over the world. London. Seoul. Dallas. Tokyo. She's only forty-one years old and already had a stack of closed cases. With indictments. And convictions. White-collar money fraud her specialty. Including counterfeit crews. I was impressed. Hell, I was stunned.

So what the hell was she doing that day in my office? That bad-dream act she pulled in my office was obviously an under-cover operation. A con of the first magnitude. And convincing. She sure made me believe it, hungover or not. But why me? What could I possibly have to do with an international counterfeit or money laundering ring? Clearly she wanted me to have that money. To ascertain if was bogus, maybe? Trying to launder it by having me go out spend it? How could that even possibly work? Or just stash it with me, maybe? Hide it from someone. That made no sense either. US Secret Service can do that all on their own. Unless . . .

It hit me like a hammer fist to the temple. A slap upside the head. A face plant. Things started to fall into place like those little blocks in Tetris. Faster and faster they stacked up as revelation after revelation flooded Mr. Brain. The supernotes! She's tracking supernotes! How could I not see it before? Was I just getting old? A rogue element within the CIA had to be using bona fide Treasury plates, inks, fabrics, and the actual printers to print American hundred-dollar bills. Bogus bills. But it was real fake money. Real in the sense that it was indistinguishable from Treasury money. They used the same plates, same printer, same inks, same cutters, same fabric. Fake because it wasn't sanctioned by the Treasury and never made it to the Federal Reserve Banks. And I was in possession of ninety-nine of them. And Nick probably still had one.

OK, fine. I get it. But what did all that have to do with me? What possible benefit could I have to her tracking supernotes? I still couldn't make the connection.

OK, so our gal Maggie St. James was covert. On the trail of an insider CIA counterfeit money operation. Damn! An op like that had to be blacker than black. Like the revelation of a frozen alien corpse locked up at Area 51. Or of alien outposts on the moon. That kind of black. I began to appreciate John and David's conspiratorial paranoia. Couldn't be more than a handful of agents on that counterfeiting crew. This operation was definitely lurking in the belly of the beast. Hiding in plain sight. Well, it's been said that the safest place is in the heart of danger.

Central Intelligence Agency.

Holy shit.

I leaned back in my chair and plopped my alligator boots up on the desk. Stared up at the ceiling fan wheezing away. Engaged in pranayama. Structured breathing. Slow inhale. Fill the lungs. Hold. Exhale slowly. Hold. Do it again. To quiet and clear Mr. Brain. And relax Mr. Jake. We both needed to focus.

OK, we have the what. And the who. Now, the why. Why did they come to ol' Jake Randall, half-assed, broke-down, semi-retired private eye? I do insurance fraud, missing persons. Brainless surveillance and lame cases like that. International intrigue and money laundering required a certain a skill set I didn't possess. And it was way above my pay grade.

So that means there had to be a personal connection. Of me and her. Or me and whoever was making funny money. More probably me and her. The BOLO had come to me at Collier after all. She had poked me twice now. So I had to have some connection to her. Directly. At some time and in some place. There's no other reason why they would come to me otherwise. That I knew of, at least.

I pulled the laptop screen closer to me. Kept reading her file.

I checked the dossier again for any aliases she may have ever used. There were several. Regina MacArthur. Kate Jordan. Elizabeth Cottingham. All regal sounding Anglo-Saxon names. None rang a bell. No pictures of her in disguise, either. I didn't expect undercover stuff to be in her Secret Service file, but I had to check anyway. I checked her DOB. She's twenty some-odd years younger than me. Young enough to be my daughter. That leaves out us being in school together somewhere along the line. Hell, I had retired the first time before she was even born. Maybe I knew her parents. St. John? Didn't ring a bell. But was that even her real name? It had to be. Federal operators' files always carry the birth name. The legal name. So I was reasonably sure of that being her real name. Could be her married name, maybe. She probably wasn't married, though, considering her line of work. But who knows, these days. She could have married her partner. Was she connected to somebody I arrested down in Collier

County? Maybe. Again the name just wasn't ringing any bells.

Frank and I had lots of collars, chasing bales of weed and bricks of coke being flown into the vast remote areas of the Everglades. Usually from Columbia or Nicaragua. All or most of those perps we busted had Spanish surnames, though. Nothing remotely British or Anglo like St. James or any of her other aliases. Besides, if she was somehow connected to any of those Collier County arrests, Frank would have remembered. And if he did, he would have said something. And he hadn't. So if she was a connection to me, and not through the Collier County days, then when? And how? Mr. Brain was digging through his ancient memory achieves, but no St. John was coming up. St. John. I would surely remember that.

The pranayama was working. Mr. Brain was getting oxygen. I was sorting things out. We still needed clarity.

I tried another tack.

There's a bookcase in my office that has all kinds of volumes in it. Books I've owned forever. I use it for reference material, but I keep it around mostly because it makes me look scholarly and well read. Some literary classics for show; Oxford English Dictionary, also mostly for show; some law school books; a set of current Florida Statutes for reference; and some other stuff just to take up shelf space. Like crystal decanters.

And like yearbooks.

I decided to give it a try. It was thin. I was grasping. But I had to chase down any and all leads.

It couldn't be that easy. What the hell. I found my high school yearbooks that hadn't been opened in decades. Pulled down the most recent, my senior year, and blew the dust off. Flipped it open. God. The hairstyles in those days. I started with seniors in my graduating year. Thumbed through the senior graduate pages. No St. John. Past all the junior classes. No St. John. Then the superlatives pages. Football. Sports.

Chess club. Academic. On and on. Nothing. Past the clubs and sports pages and . . . ahh. Wait. Here we go. Exchange students. India, China, France, Poland, and England. We apparently had a lot of exchange students back then. Funny. I didn't remember a single one.

England. And then there he was. Ian Rupert St. John: Manchester, Northwestern England. Un-fucking-believable.

The decades-old picture wasn't completely recognizable as Messr. Astor, but it certainly could be him. I didn't pay much attention to him at the time, especially when I had that beautiful dame to study. But the name clinched it. But it was his, not hers. Her dad, maybe? I left that coincidence unresolved for the moment. I continued. He had to be the dame's escort. The guy that came in the office and picked her up. He had to be part of the con too. But in no way was it just a coincidence. I had Mr. Brain access my archived high-school memories while I kept working out the connection of both of them to me.

Then it all came back to me in a rush. Late middle 1960s, British invasion rock. Manchester, Leeds, and Liverpool. Like me, he played trumpet in the school marching band. Seventh period, senior year. He was in a garage band, too, like me. Not in my band, but in another one with some other friends of mine. It came rushing back. Mr. Brain was proud to have found the memories filed deeply in his archive. In the school band, I played first-chair trumpet, and Rup was trumpet third chair. After school we all had our own rock and roll garage bands. I was the rhythm guitarist in my band, and he was a seriously good keyboardist in his. And since band was the last class of the day, we—he and I and a bunch of other budding rock and rollers—used to jam in the band room for hours. God, that was fun. That was high school, full of youthful euphoria. When everyone's group was going to be the next

Beatles or Stones. My band lasted two years, I think. Cut one record. He went back to Manchester after graduation. Don't know what happened to him after that. Or his band.

But it was all beginning to come back. In British aristocracy, St. John is pronounced something like Sin-Jen. At least he pronounced it that way. I only knew him as Rup. With a long U. It's no wonder I couldn't place St. John at first. But how was he connected to our Miss Maggie? Her father maybe? The age difference would be about right. And she did have a slightly aristocratic accent, slightly British.

But if that was their connection to me, it was thin. Wafer thin. It made exactly no sense. I hadn't seen him in nearly fifty years. But it was something. I sat back down, propped my boots up, and continued with the deep breathing.

Meditation and raja yoga are my secret weapons. They allow me to think outside the box. Tennessee whisky is my crutch. It allows me a reprieve from the world. At least that's how I define my virtues and vices. After this minor success, I deserved a reward.

What I wanted was a drink. What I needed was more pranayama.

I went with the latter.

Deep thinking—and by that I mean consciously altering one's own brain wave patterns—burns calories. A lot of calories. When applied and controlled it supports and enhances intelligence. Increases IQ. It's true. It may appear to a casual observer that I was in a state near sleep. Dozing, maybe. Or napping. Leaned all the way back in my high-back leather chair. Boots propped up on the recently cleared oak desk. Eyes closed. Breathing rhythmically. But sleep was nowhere near. I was in a self-induced alpha state. That's a brainwave frequency that is lower than waking, but higher than normal sleep. An altered but controlled state of mind. Heightened cosmic awareness.

Zen squared.

Mr. Brain was doing some heavy mental lifting. Deep squats, it felt like. Maximum weight.

The exercise allows the normal internal mental dialogue of the inane and mundane to be turned off. Mr. Brain could tune into the cosmic background of Jungian consciousness uninhibited. There was no static in the attic. My Anja chakra began to tingle and enlarge. That's the sixth one, located in the forehead between the eyes. The so-called third eye. It connects neurologically to the pineal gland located deep in the brain. To see the unseen. To expose hidden truths. I began to see the answers to the questions I had.

It was working. It always does.

I was replaying everything that had happened so far in this insane and surreal case. Trying to tie it up. Make sense of it. Take personalities out of the equation. Replace with facts and motivations. I was a detective. Time to detect. Not merely to wonder. Or guess. Awareness of the unknown was the goal. It was working.

Something much like a new galaxy was starting to form in that ever expanding vastness of my universal consciousness. My eyes are closed, but I clearly see it in my Heads Up Display. The HUD of the mind. The mental screen. That's how it comes together. Facts and motivations start to congeal and then orbit around what would become a self-contained system. That system, when fully formed, would be the case itself. Pure, interactive, and perfect. That was my goal. To see the complete set of events manifest into a perfect three-dimensional solution.

Some people view a vexing problem in need of a solution as a jigsaw puzzle. Two dimensionally. But I see it as a three-dimensional formation coming together, floating in the ether. Like a visual depiction of a new solar system forming. A star forming from plasma gas, its gravity pulling planets into its orbit. Or I see it as the chemical formation of a molecule, to use a different but applicable metaphor. It's 3D and in living color. Vivid. Two hydrogen atoms attracting an oxygen atom and then uniting to form a water molecule. Revolving in HUD space like a computer's screen saver image. Then attracting another oxygen atom to form a hydrogen peroxide compound. Metaphorically it was like that. Facts of the case were as atoms, or planets, and the final solution would become the molecular compound, or a solar system. When complete, the facts would support the solution. Visually. Yet it was a highly intuitive process.

Whether micro or macro, molecular or galactic, the universe behaves the same as it forms and grows.

I call it the molecular theory. This was my visual metaphor as it pertained to solving cases.

I remembered what Nick had said about counterfeiters. The best foreign-made bogus paper came from individual crews working out of North Korea and England. And the CIA counterfeiting operation stateside. And there really is a Treasury printing complex in Dallas. Enter domestic paper. Well, now. England and Korea. And Texas. I couldn't shake the notion that all this bogus currency had to be coming from a rogue element within the CIA. It fit the theory. Only the CIA would have the access, plant and material, and the skills needed to produce supernotes. I was heavily leaning in that direction. But I had to chase all the leads. Be thorough. Detect. Three leads. And I had a connection to two of the three. As far as I knew. Maybe all three. The dame—our dear Miss Maggie—may be a Brit, and her escort—now known to me as Rup—was obviously British. And Korea was like an atom forming in my mental molecule. The attractor at the center. Other facts were attracted and fell into orbit around that. A molecule was born. And I had a connection to Korea. It was well known. But my connection was to South Korea, not North. The Texas thing had to be rogue CIA elements. And I was somehow at the center. That's how this whole case came waltzing into my half-assed, broke-down detective agency office.

I was calm and serene when I opened my eyes. Going into an alpha brain wave state is healthy. And it's useful when solving vexing problems and situations.

It had worked again. I may have solved the case. It was so obvious to me now.

Now all I had to do was prove it.

I realized I was hungry.

Mr. Brain had burned a lot of calories.

And I didn't even want a drink.

CHAPTER SEVEN

Politics is a dirty business. It lacks purity. It's corrosive. Things are rarely as they seem. I say that because however strong a belief system is, however dedicated to an ideology one is, one always has to lie down with the enemy. That corrupts. And it's vile. Yet it's necessary.

I remember the times Frank and I went undercover to bust South American drug smugglers. The Glades was both their debarkation and destination. Fly shit in. Fly US currency out. For us to be convincing, it was necessary to fully immerse in the role. Frank is half Cuban so it was no effort for him. He spoke Spanish fluently with flair. But, for me, I had to actually become the Anglo drug buyer. Not just act the part, but actually intellectually become a distributor. Method acting, I think it's called. In the dark unchartered vastness of the Everglades, we'd meet unauthorized midnight flights from God knows where. Columbia. Nicaragua. Small planes landing in desolate and abandoned roadways deep in the Glades. Offload coke and weed. Exchange for cash. We bought dozens of kilos of llello—the Spanish pronunciation sounds like *yay-yo*— and tons of ganja with federal money in order to create credibility with these lowlifes. Uneducated, vicious, and worthless bastards. Always knowing that the money was going to further their unholy enterprise. At least the drugs we bought weren't getting on the street. They'd go directly into evidence rooms. But we weren't their only customers. Not a day went by that I didn't want to shove my .45 in their mouths, pull the trigger, and blow the back of their heads out. With extreme prejudice. But I didn't. We smiled, we laughed, we snorted line after line of un-stepped-on coke right next to them. All in the guise of undercover law enforcement. It was dirty business. In the end, we got them. Killed most, imprisoned some . . . the rest got away. But we got them and their drugs off the street. Mostly. We won. But snorting llello is long-term suicide; it will kill you sooner or later. I've seen it happen. And I could never wash that drug-dealer stink off me.

Politics is like that. I get it. After the attack of 9/11, the administration built an international coalition dedicated to fighting the Global War on Terror. Noble effort. The world united against Muslim Islamic terrorists. That's what the stated goal was and still is. But look closely at those allied member nations. Several are the very purveyors of Islamic jihad, either directly or in a supporting role. We—the US government— know that, yet we pretend they're on our side. Worse, they pretend to be on ours. It's a farce. It's all for show. We kill jihadists, but they just rearm new recruits and strike again. With fresh materiel and supplies from "friendly" nations.

And once a year, we sit down and eat with them. It's creepy mingling with those vicious bastards.

But that's how I got to know Colonel Park Sung-Ki, South Korean Army, tour of duty CENTCOM, International Coalition War on Terror.

The headquarters for the global war on terror is through the United States Central Command. And CENTCOM is located on Tampa's MacDill Air Force Base. That's in my backyard. Tampa is a military town, among other things, and enjoys a great symbiotic relationship with the military. That creates many opportunities for civilians like me to interact with officers and diplomats of the twenty or so "allied" member nations for which CENTCOM is responsible. These are the fighters against Muslim extremism. These nations are primarily from the Middle East, North Africa, and Central Asia. Many were Muslim majority nations. I didn't trust them, even though they were here in the US to fight radical Islamic jihad. Along with our solid allies in Western Europe, they got US government security clearance. Unbelievable. Rebecca Lynn is a major player in the legal community in the Tampa Bay area and, as such, she's invited to CENTCOM exclusive events. By invitation only. Not for the common man. Security is tight. You have to be invited, and you have to be vetted and cleared. And you can't come armed. Which both she and I always are. But not here. All arising from the international politics in the war on terror.

One of these events is the annual Coalition dinner. I call it a dinner, but it's actually a showcase of national cuisine from coalition member nations. International buffet. No tables, no chairs. Paper plates and plastic glasses. Coalition members in traditional dress, showcasing their traditional food. It's held in one of the huge hangers on MacDill Air Force Base.

We always go to these things together. She's a foodie and wants to sample everything. I like to chat up the military officers and diplomats from these foreign nations. Drink French wine. And English ale. Eat Oriental food. That's how I met Colonel Park Sung-Ki, South Korean Army. He and I got to know each other over the years. I've even had his family over to the house for a traditional American Thanksgiving dinner a couple of times. A good man.

My metaphysical insight suggested to me that he was possibly involved with the counterfeiting operation. Nick had said one counterfeiting op was run out of North Korea. Sung-Ki was from South Korea. It was thin. I didn't have all the details yet. But I did have the big picture. England and Korea. And I trusted my insight. It had come through for me more than once. But I was pissed. I liked Sung-Ki: He's an intelligent, engaging and insightful guy. A perfect diplomat. Right. Perfect for injecting bogus currency into the nation's M1 monetary flow. What had Nick said? Three and a half million bucks in bogus funny money coming out of Korea. Or was it England? Didn't matter. It was a sobering revelation that he might be involved. I really liked the guy. But was he dirty? If so, I had to take him down. He would have diplomatic immunity. Not to mention security clearance up the ass to be involved with CENTCOM. With diplomatic immunity, no law could take him down. Only killing him would work. But to do that, I would have to find a way to go through channels. Back channels. It'd be tough. Nearly impossible.

He spotted me from across the hanger. Waved. I waved back. Headed over to the Korean display where he was standing. He was behind the counter helping the traditionally dressed Korean girls serve Kimchi and Gogi gui to the crowd. Hot spicy cabbage and marinated barbeque pork. He personally handed me a plate. A gesture of respect. I took it with both hands. Slight head bow. Respect acknowledged and returned. Formality out of the way, he motioned for me to come around the serving table and to the back of the hanger. Where we could talk. We chatted. Small talk while I tried to eat.

Rebecca Lynn was over in the French section getting another red wine.

I put down the now empty paper plate. Wiped my mouth. The Gogi gui was superb.

"Got a question for you."

I decided to roll the dice. Take a risk. What's the worst that could happen? Bad decisions make more good stories.

Sung-Ki smiled and nodded expectantly.

"Sure."

I handed him one of the hundred-dollar bills I got from Maggie.

"Check this out. Know where I can get more of these?"

Shit. I fucked it up. I was clumsy. Didn't set it up properly. I knew it the second I said it. But I was committed now.

His tour of duty at CENTCOM would be just twenty-four months. And he had been on station for a year already. He was just now beginning to recognize—if not fully understand—American idioms.

I watched his reaction carefully. He took the bill and looked at it quizzically. Turned it over a couple of times. Looked up at me.

He paused a beat. Cocked his head. Then his face exploded into a big smile, and he laughed.

"Ah! I get it. That's funny, Jake. You want to get more of these. Ha! Yeah, me too! Me, *too!*"

I watched his eyes closely for any hint of recognition of the bill. Or disingenuousness. My eyes silently probed him. Old-style US hundred-dollar bill. Is it your work?

Asians are a tough read. Inscrutable. But I saw nothing suspect. Maybe confusion. Crazy goddamn Americans, he was probably thinking.

I laughed with him. Pretended it was a joke. Just one he didn't get.

"That's very funny, Jake. You're very funny."

I just shrugged. He handed me the bill.

"No, that's OK. You can keep it."

He looked at me strangely. Like he was surprised. Or shocked. It made no sense to him, I'm sure. Koreans just don't go around giving away hundred-dollar bills. Especially for a bad joke. I didn't care. I got one hundred of them for listening to a loony dame's bad dream, so I figured it was a perfect reward for him. And it served as my penitence for my guilt of thinking he had anything to do with counterfeiting. And, after all, the bill was probably worthless. Even if it wasn't, well, it was his to keep either way. Something to remember me by.

He smiled strangely at me again and just shook his head.

But he stuffed it in his pocket just the same.

Rebecca Lynn saved me. She came over with a fresh wine in one hand.

"Hi, Colonel Park. So good to see you again. How's Mi-Sun?"

"She's fine, Rebecca. Thanks for asking."

"She's such a lovely wife."

She turned to me.

"Her name means beauty and goodness. Isn't that lovely?"

I smiled and nodded. Sung-Ki just grinned. We'd had this conversation several times before. Sung-Ki and Mi-Sun and their two daughters had been guests in our house on several occasions. And twice for Thanksgiving dinners. I guess Rebecca Lynn just liked to say Korean names and savor their lyrical timbre.

Rebecca Lynn turned back to Colonel Park.

"Is she here tonight?"

"No, sorry. Not tonight."

"Pity. I would have very much liked to have seen her. Give her my best, won't you?"

Without missing a beat, she continued.

"Did y'all see the hookah pipes at the Jordanian display? Or maybe it was in the Saudi Arabia section. Oh, and I met one of the Saudi princes. He seemed kind of old to still be only a prince."

She snickered at her little dig. I knew the guy she was

speaking about. He and I shared war stories a little earlier.

She kept on.

"Anyway, they're huge and made of solid brass. The hookahs, I mean. And they have real Turkish tobacco."

She gestured in the general direction of the Jordan and Saudi Arabia displays with her glass. Wine sloshed on the hanger floor.

Sung-Ki and I nodded and acted interested. The awkward moment between us had been dispelled, at least. The three of us chatted about the coalition food and drinks. And about when we would get together again. I was disappointed that the lead I thought I had turned out to be nothing. Bad actors in the Koreas may have printed bogus bills, but I was now convinced that Sung-Ki had nothing to do with it. He wasn't even aware of any counterfeiting. That really wasn't his military occupational specialty after all. Fighting Islamic terrorists was. But I was glad he seemed not to be in the counterfeit-money distribution business. I felt guilty thinking he had anything to do with it. I just hope I wasn't wrong. I'm usually right. And I hoped this was one of those times.

I needed a drink. Libations were in order. Even with all the Muslim countries represented here, you could still rely on the United Kingdom, Canada, France, Australia, New Zealand, and Spain to offer some delightful libations. Their wines, ales, and spirits all made palatable adult beverage samples. And they contained alcohol. They were good and true allies. The United States kiosk only served Coke. It was deemed politically correct to not serve alcohol in the presence of all these Muslim countries. I get it. We're the host country. Tennessee whisky or even Kentucky bourbon would be more appropriate. Or at least a few California wines or American beers. But, no. We had to be accommodating and politically correct.

At least Coke was better than Pepsi.

It still pissed me off, though.

I headed in that general direction, toward those nations serving drinks. Had Rebecca Lynn in tow. She seemed to be in a reasonably good mood. Couple more drinks and we'll blow this joint.

If I could get her home before she drank too much or passed out or went to sleep on the drive home; well, it had been a long time. I was more than ready.

Fifteen minutes later I began guiding her toward the massive hanger doors and out onto the parking area on the tarmac. She wasn't resisting.

Thanks, Lord.

Lucky, Jake. Just stay lucky.

I did.

* * *

Morning came early the next day. And it was a good day too. We had a tender moment last night, a bonding that we hadn't shared in, well, to me it seemed like forever. She was singing in the shower when I went to make coffee. I was in a good mood. So was she. We chatted aimlessly at breakfast with each other. It was something we had not done in a while. The crossword went unsolved. Newsgroups unread. It was good.

Later, with Rebecca Lynn off to her office to interview another client and begin her day, well, I headed for the office.

David was already in his office when I came in. Early morning was something David wasn't usually acquainted with. Nonetheless, I nodded my morning greeting as I walked past his office door. Headed down the hall to mine. I had barely settled in when David come in and folded himself into one of my overstuffed chairs. Leg thrown over the arm. His usual posture. Millennial casual.

"Guess what?"

David never fails. Always starts a conversation that way. And he never makes coffee at the office. All the necessaries are there: Coffee pot, gourmet coffee properly ground, clean cups, and sugar and cream. Even honey. He just doesn't *make* coffee. That's why I always have to make my own. For the first cup anyway. I sat down, propped my alligator boots up on the desk. Took a long pull on my Dunkin' Donuts French Vanilla coffee. Hot and freshly made. Light and sweet. Eyed him. Prolonged the usual ritual.

"Bucs won?"

David snorted. It was our usual repartee.

"Remember I told you Bob Dylan got shot?"

I nodded. Dylan again. What now?

"It was a fake news thing."

Oh. Well, then. That explains it.

David lives for the attention. You always have to prompt him.

"Fake in what way?"

"OK, listen. This is great."

David was getting warmed up. Now that he had an audience. He sat forward in his chair.

"He was doing an impromptu gig in Greenwich Village—a live performance of just a few tunes—and ended the set with 'Knocking on Heaven's Door.' Well, during the last chorus and fade, there was a gunshot as part of the song. It was actually just the drummer doing a rim shot, and Dylan dropped to one knee as the song ended and the lights faded to black. Pretty cool on the video. You know the song, right?

He sang it. Or tried. I just looked at him.

"I know the song."

He continued.

"Well, it was just stagecraft, you know, but some messed-up stoned yoo-hoo in the crowd immediately tweeted a photo of Dylan supposedly getting shot while on stage. And Yahoo is on Twitter, so they picked it up . . . and it went viral. Yahoo thought they had a scoop and ran with it. Can you believe that? I mean, like, everybody fell for it. Even me. And that's when I told you. But they had to publicly retract it on Twitter and again in today's morning newsfeed. Dylan's people called them up and politely asked them just what exactly they thought they were doing. Even Dylan tweeted something like 'The news of my demise has been greatly exaggerated.' Oh, man, it's priceless! Anyway, that's where I saw the actual video."

I wondered briefly if David knew Dylan was apparently paraphrasing Mark Twain.

He paused and looked at me expectantly. I guess I was supposed to applaud. I didn't.

Mr. Brain was shaking his head at the absurdity of it all.

Dylan's in a bad dream. Dylan auctions off a belt. Dylan's dead. No, Dylan's fine. He's resurrected. Jesus. I was seriously over anything Dylan. And Yahoo News.

"Huh."

"Yeah, fake news is something, isn't it?"

"Huh."

"Well, I thought you'd want to know, you being a big Dylan fan and all. You looked, like, pretty psyched about it the other day."

"Oh, yeah. Yeah, thanks. No, that's all good news. Good to know."

I eyed him for another moment. Took another pull on my coffee. What could I say? I'm no Dylan fan. Not in the least. Especially of his early stuff. Lyrically it was passable, maybe. But no introspective nasal whining for me, thanks. No, I'm an aging baby-boomer hard-core rock and roller. Give me a beat in four-four time with a shuffle rhythm. Buzz distortion guitar and twelve-bar, three-chord blues progressions. Yeah. That's what I'm talking about.

But I was relieved. The bad Dylan dream just retreated back into a psychotic dame's dark and bloody fantasy. Where it belonged. And out of my reality. It was starting to become a pretty good day. Actually, an even better day. I thought about Rebecca Lynn and last night. And had to smile in spite of myself.

Hell, I felt great.

David was talking about other non-news news as I was reliving my tender moments last night with Rebecca Lynn. Mr. Brain kept on working, digesting David's most recent Dylan news.

Then John came in.

"Hey, guys, take a look at this."

David looked up from the overstuffed. John came over to my desk and showed me a news article on his tablet screen. David got up and looked over John's shoulder, squinting at the tablet. The story was about some felony charges that the FBI had brought up against Amir Shelby.

I had no idea who he was.

John was eager to tell us.

"He's the chairman of the Florida state chapter of CAIR."

He looked at us both for a sign of recognition.

He didn't find one. He went on.

"Oh, OK. Well, he's a big shot in the Council on American-Islamic Relations. CAIR. State level. Office is in Tampa."

More blank states.

John was exasperated.

"Guys, it's a Muslim group that vigorously challenges anything they perceive to be a negative Islamic stereotype. Think ACLU for Muslims. The United Nations has designated them as a terrorist outfit, as has certain elements of the US government. Like the Muslim Brotherhood is a terrorist outfit. Actually, CAIR is the Brotherhood's political propaganda arm; they're one and the same. They promote all things Islam, counter what they call Islamaphobia, and aggressively sue anyone who, in their opinion, slams it. This guy is their state chairman. The FBI has had him on their radar, apparently, for some time. And he got arrested with a laptop in his possession full of pedophilia, child porn, and bestiality. There're even some videos, apparently of him, actually fucking a goat and laughing."

John snickered at that. Shook his head. David and I looked at each other. My morning coffee was still warm, so it was way too early to conjure up mental images of a raghead fucking a goat. Even Mr. Brain gagged.

John continued with his story.

"Well, he's a big shot in a powerful lobbying group, so he basically skated on the charges. And of course the Muslim community is all in a rage about his arrest. He had some inside political pull, apparently. Seems the feds couldn't quite prove that it was his laptop and, therefore, he's not responsible for what may be on it. Case dismissed. That's what the judge in the article said anyway. But from the between-the-lines reporting, it seems he really is one sick puppy. I mean, boinking little kids and goats? That's seriously messed up. Somebody should just castrate this bastard."

David looked nonplussed. Mr. Brain wanted a change in subject matter.

I took another pull on my coffee.

John thumbed through a few screens and found another article.

"Here's another guy that merits a mention, filed under anti-American rhetoric."

He turned the tablet so David and I could see it. It was

a YouTube video of a radical Muslim cleric named Rashid al-Mubarak being introduced at a sharia rally in Tampa a few years ago.

John continued.

"He had come over from the Middle East to give one of his fiery speeches. To incite the local Islamic community to jihad through adherence to the insane and vicious seventh-century Koran. It was culturally revealing to me to actually hear parts of his speech and what he was actually saying. Kill all homosexuals; women are essentially just men's chattel; Jews must be killed on sight; and Christians must be converted, killed, or made dhimmi and enslaved. And more and more seventh-century desert tribalistic sharia law ad nauseum. He demanded sharia law be implemented in place of the Constitution and Bill of Rights right now. Revolt against America, the Great Satan. I was stunned. Open sedition right here on US soil!"

John paused and shook his head in exasperation. But he went on.

"I had never given Islam a second thought before this. And I certainly no idea that Islam's leaders were actually inciting that kind of hateful, violent insurgency against the US, its government, and its culture. Especially against Western white people. It was unnerving. And rude. Never mind that the US is their host country. They want to burn it all down. Well, what the hell. That's freedom of speech for you."

I was about to turn away from the video when it jump cut back to the very first part of the rally. A local Muslim businessman was introducing this cleric al-Mubarak. I caught his name—Awad—because it reminded me of a rude schoolyard slur. According to the voice-over on the video, apparently this guy had been in the news before. I looked at John questioningly.

John explained his name was Hassan Mahajir Awad, an

Egyptian national who had come to Tampa in the early 2010s and bought several halal delis around the Tampa Bay area. I remembered there was even one on US 19 in Clearwater. I hadn't ever eaten there; that's just not my fare. But I noticed it because the business sign was written in Arabic. I had no idea what halal even was.

Back on the video, Awad was a microphone hound. He went on and on about what a great mullah this Rashid al-Mubarak was, how learned, and how sharia law was God's only true word. He actually said Allah, but I got the drift. He was fat, wore a blue blazer over an open shirt, and his long black hair was slicked straight back. All that coupled with the three-day beard growth and sweat glistening on his forehead made him look kinda sleazy and greasy. And his appearance actually accentuated his anger and rage. It showed.

At least he spoke English.

I looked at John and just shook my head. These guys were truly way out of touch with normal everyday American beliefs. Cultures separated by fourteen hundred years and a huge ocean. With little, if anything, in common.

If that's what Islam is all about, well, I just couldn't relate.

John nodded acknowledgement as he took back the tablet. It was still running the video. You could hear the screaming, manic and hateful fanaticism on the audio, even without seeing the video.

John looked at me and David. And offered his perspective.

"You know, I got fascinated by Islam as an ethos years ago in my comparative religions class. So I kinda keep up with what they're up to over the years. And guys, for fourteen hundred years, this is exactly the kind of destructive stuff they're always been up to. And they still are. It hasn't changed, softened, or moderated one iota in fourteen centuries. It's in no way a religious alternative to Western religions like

Judaism or Christianity. Nor even Eastern ones like Sikhism or Buddhism. It's more of an Arabic death cult—barely an ethos than a religion. I mean, one could argue that the differences between Sunni and Shia are traditionally confined to who Muhammad's preferred successor was to be, but the Wahhabism sect absolutely is a death cult. The whole belief system is just a hateful, spiteful, and jealous madman's rage against the civilized world. No other religion of any consequence promotes death and tyranny. But Islam does. It's literally insane. Kill everyone who isn't a Muslim and kill those Muslims who aren't in your sect. Dominate the entire world while enforcing a seventh-century tyrannical mindset on everyone else. And I mean everyone. And while going about all that destruction, they have not added one productive, positive thing to the cultural development of mankind. As an ethos, it has neither offered nor added anything except slavery and death to humanity."

John flipped his tablet off. Just shook his head.

I was stunned. I could see why John was qualified to teach classes.

David sighed, unimpressed, and plopped back down in the overstuffed. Politics, like sports, was beneath him too. I looked at John as he wrapped up.

"Anyway, I thought that it was all very revealing about the character traits of these supposedly civilized and concerned protectors of Islam. Didn't you?"

I had to acknowledge that I did.

"Yeah, that's all pretty messed up, all right. Now that you mention it, I have read some disturbing things about this whole radical Islam cult thing from time to time. I mean, everybody's heard of al Qaeda, but I never realized it was so pervasive. And its propaganda arm CAIR is new to me, as well. I've seen several of those beheadings and other kinds of insane videos on YouTube too. I mean, who films themselves beheading people? Didn't really know too much more about it, though."

"Yep. They are a pretty nasty insane bunch, all right."

I shook my head and turned my attention to my now cooling French vanilla coffee. John and David. My in-house purveyors of arcane news and global conspiracies.

John, who was again focusing on his tablet, pulled up his schedule. Glanced at his watch.

"Whoa. I gotta get outta here; gotta go teach my class. Catch you guys later."

He turned around and left my office.

David was hanging back. Expectantly. Probably was going to be light on the rent this month. He wanted me to give him a research task. I read him correctly.

"Uh . . . You need anything . . . ?"

I did. But I couldn't give him anything to do with Secret Service, counterfeiting, or international currency manipulation. I needed more details first. A lot more. I didn't know what I was looking for. Or even what questions to ask.

"Oh. Uh, not right now. But I'm working on some things and I might need you in a day or so."

He lit up.

"OK. Cool. Just let me know."

He untangled himself from the overstuffed and shot back out the door.

"Later."

I just lifted my coffee cup in reply.

Mr. Brain wanted me to get back to the real issues at hand. I thought it was a good idea too.

If I were a missing Secret Service agent, and I was in Clearwater meeting with a detective, and my handlers sent a missing persons alert to said detective's last known place of employment, where would I be? What would I be doing? Or, if I was running a con under those criteria, what would be my next move? Those were the questions running around in my head. Or maybe it's all just a smoke screen, designed to obfuscate and obscure an obvious fact. I couldn't tell. Yet. My metaphorical molecule had cleared any possible connection I might have had with the Korea lead. It died and went nowhere. One down. Two to go. The next obvious lead was Maggie St. John.

And I hadn't figured that angle out yet.

I just wished Marie had come in today. I wanted to bounce this loony-dame-Dylan-bad-dream psychosis off her. It was pathological, and that was Marie's field of expertise. I knew she'd have an angle I hadn't considered. But she only came into the office when she had patients or needed to catch up on clerical work. I guess she was off again today. Damn.

I could hear David's keyboard clacking away in his office down the hall. I was still trying to decide if there was anything to this whole Dylan thing. Or if I should give David something to research. But I was sure Dylan was just a distraction. Nothing there. Just some dame's loony dream. Then I heard the front door wind chimes. Glanced at my watch. Mail, probably.

I heard Reggie coming down the hall. He usually just leaves all the mail on the receptionist's desk. But today he came down the hall, past the receptionist's desk. All the way back to my office.

I actually had a receptionist once. Some twentysomething cutie. Shapely brunette with a vivacious personality. Very smart, outgoing, and engaging. Eye candy for the office. Gave the place a professional office ambiance. Greeted guests, answered all the phones, made coffee. And she did my books and dealt with my business's minutia. With her there, I charged a little more rent for the extra service. But then I had to pay her a salary and put up with all the bullshit that employees inevitably create. What I wanted was a cute, vivacious, and professional receptionist up front. What I got was drama, chaos, and headaches. So now I don't have a receptionist.

But at least there's a desk up front.

Reggie popped into my office with his electronic signature module and a small package.

"Package for you today, boss. You been doing all right?"

"Barely keeping out of trouble, Reg. What we got here?"

"Sign here, and it's all yours to find out."

I scribbled on the small screen and took the package and the mail.

Reggie was eyeing my signature and making notes on his module as he headed back up the hall.

"See ya, Reggie. Be careful out there."

"Oh, yeah. You can count on it!"

I heard David leave with him as he shouted back over his shoulder.

"See ya, Jake. I'm outta here."

I nodded and raised an arm in a silent response.

Shuffling through the pile, I sorted all the tenants' mail and stacked it in neat separate piles to one side on my desk. Made another pile of mine. Looked at the package. No return address. Opened it.

And sat down in disbelief.

Inside the small box was a pink drink umbrella with *Sword and Shield* printed on it. The same one I got on my first date with Rebecca Lynn. And the same one I gave the dame with the bad Dylan dream. The loony dame who I now know is actually Maggie St. John, United States Secret Service.

And now I have it back.

My what-the-fuck meter pegged into the red. Again. Mr. Brain was babbling to himself incoherently. I was just thinking about starting to seriously look for her, and I instantly get this. More dharma.

The universe trying to get my attention. Or laughing. Either way, better listen up.

In the box along with the umbrella was a handwritten post-it note that said simply,

Find me yet? –msj.

MSJ. Maggie St. John. Cute. She's teasing me. Again. After buying her bad dream act, I guess I am an easy mark. OK, fair game. Gauntlet thrown.

I sat down in my chair and plopped my boots up on the desk. Pondered the little pink umbrella. Held it up in my hand and twirled it around. Hoping some degree of Jungian cosmic consciousness would seep epidermically into my fingers, then into Mr. Brain. He could use some help.

The universe decided it couldn't help me just yet.

I got nothing.

What I wanted was to be rid of this case and its nagging bizarre twists.

What I got was more nagging bizarre twists.

But then the universe changed its mind.

I heard the wind chimes on my office door tinkling away. Tinkling longer than normal. Either someone was coming in, like *really* coming in, or there were more than one entering my humble, half-assed, broke-down private detective's office.

I checked Mr. Kimber tucked in my holster on my hip. I was in condition one, cocked and locked. The thumb break was in place behind the slide, in front of the hammer. Everything was as it should be. I had seven .45 caliber rounds in the magazine, one in the pipe. Safety on. Eight on my side.

Still in my chair, with boots on the desk, I waited for whoever it was to come through my office door. I didn't have to wait long.

She stopped and stood in my doorway for a just beat. My mouth dropped open.

It was the drop-dead gorgeous Dylan dreaming dame. Maggie St. John, United States Secret Service was back in my office.

She smiled at me.

That thousand-watt smile.

CHAPTER EIGHT

"Hello, Jake. Looks like you found me."

Found her? I'd been thrashing around just trying to keep my head above water in this bizarre fucking case. And not being entirely successful at it. I was in over my head. Now she walks into my office. Again. So finding her was all her. It was a gift.

"May I come in?"

Mr. Brain was trying hard to find something to say. Anything. I think I must have stood up. Guys go all mushy and stupid when in the presence of a beautiful dame with hazel-green eyes and red lips. And a thousand-watt smile. I croaked out something like an invitation to come on in. It sounded like an old dog barking. I flailed my arm toward the overstuffed. I hope she remembered it.

I was stunned and confused, and Mr. Brain was missing in action. He was hiding under the bed. And I needed a drink.

And then it got worse.

Messr. Astor appeared at the door. The same guy that had retrieved her before. I never got his name, so that's what I named him. All aristocratically British, tailored clothes, plumy accent. This time he was smiling like he knew something I didn't. I was sure he did. It wouldn't have been hard.

Maggie addressed him over her shoulder.

"Come in, Uncle Rupert."

Uncle Rupert? My what-the-fuck-meter was still pegged in the red. The needle was bent. Trying to go off the gauge.

"Jake, I want you to meet my uncle, my dad's brother, Mr. Rupert St. John with British Security Service. Uncle Rupert, Jake Randall. You've met him once before, as I'm sure you'll recollect."

"Hello, Jake. Long time, then, eh?"

I just stared. It couldn't be. The memory of Rup the key-boardist in high school, the photo in the yearbook, all was superimposed and overlaid with the vision of the regal chap standing before me. I could now see the metamorphosis that had occurred over the last forty-five or so years. Everyone ages, I guess.

He was looking at me in the same way.

When one's past comes blasting into one's life in an unexpected and dramatic way, it's often hard to sort out the real reality.

This was one of those times.

I stammered an acknowledgement.

"Uh . . . Rup?"

He just smiled and nodded. I plopped down into my chair. Mr. Brain was down for the count. What I wanted was to be sophisticated, urbane, and debonair. Be on their level. What I got was croaking and stuttering. I could barely process this new twist. It was overwhelming. I desperately needed a drink.

"How're . . . what's goin' . . . I . . . I mean, what can I do for you?"

They glanced at each other, sympathetic to my stunned and surprised reaction. A beautiful dame with a bad dream and her uncle I haven't seen in four decades or so come into my office. It sounded like the opening line of a bad joke. I hadn't heard the punch line yet. But I had an idea of what it would be.

How do you handle that?

He started to say something. Mr. Brain interrupted. I held up my hand. It couldn't be helped.

"But first, can I offer you some refreshment?"

Rup glanced around discretely but saw what I was looking at. My crystal decanter on my bookshelf.

"Oh. Quite. Yes, please. That would be lovely."

It was late morning, for Christ's sake, but for me a drink was requisite. No getting around it. I knew he was putting me at ease. This was a social call as well as business. I was beginning to remember my manners. I was as close to being a polite host as I could get just then. It would have to do. And I still desperately needed a drink.

I keep a nice crystal decanter with four matching crystal rocks glasses on a crystal tray on the third shelf of my bookcase. It's all Waterford crystal. Very expensive lead crystal. Just for showing off. In the decanter is George Dickel #12 Tennessee whisky. It's usually just for show.

Today it was medicinal.

I poured three glasses. About two ounces each. Neat. I had neither ice nor mixer. I passed them around. I took a long pull on mine, and they each sipped theirs gently. It's ninety proof. Middle of the morning. Can't be helped.

I sat back down behind my desk. Mr. Brain started to come back on line. As hungover as I was when I first met them, I had pegged them pretty much spot on. Something just not quite right. Bad dreams and psychological solutions. That's not real. They ran a con on me, I knew it, and now they've come back.

I dispensed with the normal pleasantries.

"So. I am fairly certain this has nothing to do with Bob Dylan's belt."

Rup laughed. Maggie blushed, snickered, and looked down at her lap.

"Oh, Jake. I'm so sorry about that. I had to come up with something outrageous that had no actual basis in fact. It was part of my cover. To give you a red herring to chase, as it were. To make you run around so that we could see what you might do, where you might go. And the irony is that I actually did have that dream. It was still fresh in my mind, so the story just flowed. Dreadfully sorry. The whole point of the exercise was to get that suspicious money to you. "

Then she giggled. Rup smiled. They had a secret I didn't know. Yet.

She went on.

"And you giving me that little pink drink umbrella thing? Oh my God, that was simply brilliant. Absolutely charming; you were so regal and formal with the presentation. It was precious. I was so touched. And I almost lost it laughing right then."

She laughed out loud. Hand daintily over her mouth. God, what a dame! The umbrella was still lying on my desk. They had a good laugh. I was somewhat flattered. It was a brilliant move after all, wasn't it? I chortled along with them.

Mr. Brain was not amused.

I cut her some slack. It was an explanation and an apology. And a damn good one too. God. She was magnificent. She could have said anything. It didn't matter. That smile. Those lips. Eyes. I was smitten. Make a fool of me? A couple of weeks lost chasing my tail? Almost having Mr. Brain short out? Hey, no problem. Gee, it was fun.

"Yeah. Well. Thanks."

She giggled again, and looked down. She could do no wrong. I took another sip.

Rup picked it up.

"I'm MI5, Jake. That's roughly the British equivalent of your FBI, as you're probably quite aware. Domestic intelligence. Counter terrorism branch. I—we—have been tracking a terror cell for several months. This particular cell, an offshoot of the Muslim Brotherhood, I might add, came to the UK by way of Tunisia of all places, then migrated back over the pond. To the US. Here to Florida and finally to Clearwater, in point of fact. We were concerned their target may be CENTCOM on MacDill Air Force Base in Tampa."

I nodded. Nothing was jelling yet. Pieces were not falling into place. Ends were not being tied up. Hell, I wasn't even seeing pieces yet. No molecule was formed. The Dickel was helping. I waited for more.

Rup continued.

"It seems these chaps were Muslim Brotherhood, setting up a global funding operation to support ISIS and other Muslim terror groups, including, I'm afraid, offshoots of al Qaeda, all of whom are usually at odds with each other. Our research indicated that their favorite method of raising money in order to reach their goals was to counterfeit American currency. Hundred-dollar bills to be precise. And they had some help with that through some rogue elements—true believers, I'm afraid —out of the CIA, of all places."

That struck home. Nick had mentioned CIA involvement. And I had just had a quick tutorial on the Muslim Brotherhood and Islam in general. My head snapped up when he mentioned counterfeit hundreds. Rup saw my reaction. Took a long sip on his drink. Studied the amber liquid inside. Held the glass up to me in a salute.

"I always did enjoy a good Tennessee whisky. This one is brilliant. So unlike Scotch in many ways. Very nice. Thank you, old man."

There was no label on the decanter, or anywhere else, yet

he knew it was Tennessee whisky. Bloody good show. I was impressed. The Brits are so good at diplomacy. Old man was a meant as an acknowledgment of familiarity. I smiled, raised my glass, and nodded. Mr. Brain was beginning to take copious notes. Rup nodded in reply.

But I had to ask.

"So what was the point of the ten grand you gave me? Was it bogus? Or real?"

Maggie took center stage.

"The money I gave you was taken from one of the cell members that you eliminated."

Who did I eliminate, again? Was she referring to the perps in the Boot Hill shootout?

Rup intercepted that one.

"Well, not to put too fine a point on it, but we weren't too sure about you. That's why we sent that bogus missing person BOLO down to Collier County. We were hoping it would alert your superiors down there and, in so doing, create some trepidation on your part. Rattle your cage, as it were. Possibly expose you. Make you react, to see what you might do."

Rup paused for effect, eyeing me. Then he continued.

"You were connected to the leader of the cell we were investigating after all, and we reckoned if you were bent, well, you would recognize your own work. In the bills Maggie gave you, I mean. And we hoped you'd eventually get that currency back to the cell. And expose yourself and your contacts."

Connected? How was I connected to a terror cell? Just by killing a couple of foreign wannabe rapists?

"You thought I was in cahoots with Muslim terrorists?"

"At the time it did seem plausible."

Well, now. It slowly dawned on me that the perps I shot were the same terrorists Maggie and Rup were referring to. That was a game changer. Mr. Brain sat back hard. Things were beginning to make sense.

I was glad I had a drink. I took another sip.

"But I had no idea who they really were. They were just rapists to me."

"Right. And we didn't know who you were . . . or what your motivation might be either. And here you are shooting these mutts in the middle of the night in a cemetery, of all places. Rather odd, don't you think? We assumed you had a monetary motivation to do that."

"Why would I kill those two rapists and then try to get the same cash back to the same cell? What am I missing here?"

Maggie and Rup just looked at each other.

Maggie explained it.

"Well, that's the point at which we decided you were not involved in the cell after all. You were, just as you said, a civilian stopping a gangbang."

"But you went ahead and ran that bad dream con anyway? Solely to get that counterfeit money to me? To see if I would get it back to the terrorists?"

Mr. Brain wanted those three questions answered.

But before Maggie could answer, another even more important fourth question came out of my mouth.

"And so you used me for bait?"

Rup jumped in.

"Right. That we did do. No hard feelings, old chap. It was what we thought we could work with at the time, of course, isn't it?"

"Maggie got the ten thousand dollars of counterfeit bills from Samara's effects. Those were bills that we knew were printed by rogue CIA elements we were investigating, and we decided to get it to you to see what you might do with it."

Mr. Brain was wondering who the hell Samara was.

"It turned out that you weren't involved directly with them.

By the way, do you still have it? The money, that is?"

I just nodded in the direction of my desk drawer. I didn't mention the bill I gave to Nick. Or the one to Sung-Ki. I figured Rup wouldn't care either way. Ninety-eight is as good as a hundred in bogus money.

That seemed to satisfy him.

"Right. And it was just pure happenstance that you and I were chums back in high school. By the way, do you still play? Good jams back then, wot?"

I just looked at him for a moment. Mr. Brain was doing calculations again. We were trying to keep up. It was like watching a kaleidoscope and trying to identify individual colors.

I pointed to my Taylor T-5 semi-hollow body guitar on its floor stand against the back wall of the office. It's both acoustic and electric. But I don't play it with an amplifier here in the office. You can guess why.

"Yeah. From time to time, when I can. Keeps me centered. Do you?"

Rup turned to look at the guitar and smiled.

"Oh, that's a Taylor. Damned fine guitar. My, yes, I still play. When time allots, as you can imagine."

"Yeah, me too. I guess we can never really quit."

Rup smiled at that and nodded. I tried again.

"Run this whole thing by me again. How did you think I was in any way connected to this terror cell?"

Mr. Brain wanted to know. So did I.

Maggie chimed in.

"Well, we were aware of you following them one night some weeks ago. You shot them both in a standoff during an aborted kidnapping. You killed one, and the other, one Aziz Samara, actually lived. He is—well, he *was*—the leader of that cell. You called the local police, and they came and took custody of the female victim and both our suspects' bodies. Both were either dead or wounded, so Clearwater Police Department took their prints and, as they turned out to be foreigners illegally in the US, sent them to the FBI. The FBI positively ID'd them as Muslim Brotherhood and notified Department of Homeland Security. As they were on several terror suspect lists, they were wanted by Secret Service as being counterfeiting suspects, as well as by M15 and Interpol as terror cell suspects. Really busy boys."

"The FBI called us—that is, MI5 and Secret Service, our joint task force—and asked if we wanted custody of the dead body and Samara, who, although severely wounded, as I said, managed to live. He had a vest on which stopped one round, but your second round grazed the top of the vest and took out a good part of the side of his neck. We patched him up and actually got a bit of some good intel from him. He's currently under tight security courtesy of the US government and will probably become a resident at Gitmo when he recovers."

She continued.

"Oh, by the way, the other jihadist, the one you killed, turned out to be Emir Alfarsi, a rather nasty bastard who has been videoed decapitating his victims with a knife by hand. He did a series of these so-called recruitment/terror videos for ISIS and other radical groups. His work is all over YouTube. You've seen some of them, I'm sure. He's the guy doing the cutting, standing behind the poor kneeling victim, with his fingers in their eye sockets. He has the victim's head pulled back, with their throat exposed. You've seen him, right? He's that guy."

I shuttered at the viciousness of that act. And then I nodded. Yeah, I'd seen him on those videos, all right. Recently, in fact.

Maggie kept on.

"Well, Alfarsi is one vicious evil little bastard. You saved some innocent lives by killing him in that shootout."

She paused and looked up at me.

"That was some very nice shooting by the way."

I nodded in acknowledgement. It was. Took another pull on my drink. So I shot two terrorists who were being tracked by an international task force. As they were about to gangbang some drugged-up sweet young thing. In a cemetery. All in my sleepy little city of Clearwater. Lovely.

I got up to refill my glass. Maggie passed. Rup didn't. I splashed a stout pour for each of us.

Rup continued with the briefing.

"So the fact that you and I went to school together, however briefly, played no part whatsoever in this. We were damn curious about who it was who had the opportunity to shoot and kill some suspects we were surveilling. We investigated it thoroughly. We didn't realize that you and I were classmates until we learnt who the shooter—that would be you—turned out to be. We initially thought your shootout was merely your attempt to move up in the ranks by taking out some unneeded middle management. An internal power grab as it were."

"Incidentally, the girl in question is actually the granddaughter of a Saudi prince, and she's been deported back to Saudi Arabia for her own safety. Moneyed and privileged, she's the epitome of self-absorbed devil-may-care narcissistic attitude that seems to be so pervasive in idle rich girls. She's lucky to be alive. She's fine now, we're told. We suspect that her kidnapping was a clumsy attempt to extort more money from the Saudi royal family. The House of Saud, I might add, has been funding these groups for years. We know they still are, and the US knows, and the Saudis know we know. But they do it anyway. I guess these blokes wanted more. At any rate, they most likely would have killed her anyway had you not intervened. Pity it didn't go as planned, isn't it? Bloody duplicitous Saudis."

A pity indeed. I wondered if the girl was related to my Saudi prince contact I knew from the Coalition dinner. I decided not to share that fact with them. Just yet.

Rup took a sip and smiled, then winked at me over the rim of his glass. Typical British acerbic dark humor. I loved it.

I leaned back in my chair and tried to take it all in. Mr. Brain was trying to make recognizable metaphorical molecules out of disassociated facts as they floated randomly by. He was getting there. But only just.

"I know it's quite a lot to absorb, old chap, but at least this whole bloody sordid affair is nearly over. Except for your part, that is."

Indeed it was a lot to absorb. I'm being surveilled by Secret Service and MI5. I kill two Muslim Brotherhood terrorists. The good guys think I'm one of the terrorists. I'm given ten thousand dollars in hundred-dollar bills that may be counterfeit. I'm bait for God knows what. And now I'm still not done.

"Oh? How's that?"

Maggie and Rup looked at each other. Probably trying to determine who would be elected to give me the bad news. What I wanted was this whole thing to just be over.

What I got was a new assignment. Peachy.

Maggie got the duty to tell me.

"Well, we're not done yet. We still need to weed out the bent rogues at CIA who printed these bills. And we have no way to know how much of these supernotes are getting to the Muslim Brotherhood and other terrorist groups. We think most, or possibly all of it, is going to the Brotherhood and possibly on to Hezbollah to fund their well-oiled drug dealing syndication. Clearly it must be stopped. These CIA agents are either sympathetic to—or actual members of—the Muslim Brotherhood. They're true believers: traitors, pure and simple. And we can't let CIA know what we're up to for obvious reasons. We're still not sure how high up this thing goes. The CIA always protects its own, and the upper echelon would undoubtedly muck up our investigation if they knew about it. Either way, they're not only engaged in a criminal enterprise but are complicit in conspiring with terrorists who harbor hostile intentions to the United States. So it comes down to this being a criminal enterprise, including sedition and treason."

I had a thought when she mentioned funding. I read the news, and all this triggered a memory.

"I thought the US government paid a billion and a half dollars to Iran recently. And just before that, wasn't there a pallet of four hundred million dollars in actual US currency sent to them on a US military cargo plane? Was that real, or was it this funny money?"

Rup interjected.

"That was probably real US taxpayer money, Jake. All of it, even the four hundred million."

He paused at looked at Maggie.

"That cash was supposed to go to Tehran so they would have the necessary capital to finally update their aging passenger jet fleet. The deal was to buy the planes from Boeing, as I'm sure you'll recall. At the end of the day, it turned out that all those billions were simply laundered back through the aviation unions, and ultimately back to the . . ."

"Uncle Rupert, that money was to entice Iran to go along with the nuclear deal that the previous administration wanted so badly. At least that's the official state department position after they were exposed, at any rate. We're not going to hash that out again, are we? Let's stay focused on the briefing for right now."

Rup just laughed. Looked down at the floor and smiled knowingly. He was far from dissuaded from his observation. And Mr. Brain wanted to hear the rest.

"Right. Good point. Elections do matter, do they not? So, at any rate, we don't think there's nearly that much counterfeit money out there. Not in the billions anyway. My God, if there were, that would destabilize the entire world's economy completely."

"But I thought it was so real, it is real."

Rup glanced at Maggie and shrugged.

"Well, therein lies the rub, don't you think? It's no longer a philosophical discussion, no matter how much money has been printed and put in circulation. Now it's become a matter of sedition and treason. An attempt to take down the United States—if not the whole world's economy."

"And that's pretty much a hangin' offense, isn't it?"

I was trying to be clever. It fell short. Maggie jumped in.

"Well, in a manner of speaking, yes, the terrorism part can carry a death sentence. Title 18 US code provides penalties for acts of international terrorism, and many of those include death . . . or at least a lengthy prison sentence. For the criminal side, that falls under the Attorney General's purview. That usually means FBI involvement if it's in domestic cases. But our joint task force—Secret Service and MI5, that is—has already been assigned this operation as it has many tentacles internationally, specifically in the UK, North Africa, and the US, of course. So it's all ours."

US Code. International terror cells. Rogue and bent CIA agents. Damn! I was beginning to miss those lame, boring insurance fraud cases. At least the penalty for messing those up wasn't a death sentence. And it had been a long time since I had dealt with those brutal drug lords and their mules. I was younger, then, and far more immortal. Mortally was a constant concern in my life at this point. I stood up and paced around my desk. They watched patiently. I guess they knew what I was thinking.

"So how do I fit in?"

Rup went right for the throat.

"You're the bait again, old sport."

I had been busy pacing. I stopped mid-stride and turned toward him.

"Oh. Well. That's fine, then."

That was my best shot at sarcasm. Maggie laughed, at least. Rup didn't even miss a beat.

"Right. Good show, old boy. Here's the plan. Maggie and I will go to Dallas in the morning and attempt to infiltrate the CIA printing operation there. We have some actionable intelligence now, so we're certain we can do. We will go in separately, under different covers. Further than that I cannot go, I'm sorry to say. Need to know and all that."

Yeah, need to know. That was definitely above my pay grade. I looked at Maggie. She was watching my reaction carefully. I still thought she was beautiful, even as she possibly was signing my death certificate. I waited expectantly for Rup to continue.

"The point is that you'll stay here and we will advise the rogues that you've come into some of their work, are making lots of noise about it, and they should come check you out."

I sat back down. Mr. Brain had about a half dozen questions that spilled into my consciousness chaotically. I waited expectantly. Again. That ploy seemed to be working.

Rup was up, pacing now. Hands clasped behind his back. Working through it in his head as he laid out the program. I ventured a quick question.

"Help me out. How exactly did I come into that money, again?"

Maggie intervened.

"We confiscated it from the Samara and Alfarsi takedown, of course. We got it to you hoping for a result similar to what we expect will occur when these rogue agents come for it from you."

Damn! That was so eloquently put that I had to run Mr. Brain through it one more time.

"So they'll think I got it off of Samara and Alfarsi after I killed them, right?"

Rup jumped in.

"Precisely. And at the end of the day you did, of course, didn't you?"

For effect he pointed at my desk drawer.

Ok. This is just peachy. An international task force is going to sic some rogue, bent CIA elements on me. Danger and glory. Spy versus spy. Just like in the old days with Frank. Great. But this time I'm on center stage with a lead solo. The problem is, I play rhythm.

"So what do I actually do? Sit tight? Just wait for a hit?"

Sarcasm was as forthright as I could get right now. Before I got an answer to those questions, Mr. Brain fired a few more. They went to the front of the line.

"And let me be even more frank. Exactly why do I want to do this anyway? What if I don't really want to get killed? If I just want my life back? What's in it for me?"

Rup laughed out loud. He was in full sales mode now.

"My dear boy, you're already up to your tits in this thing now, aren't you? Once the Muslim Brotherhood learns who took out their cell here stateside, savage bastards that they are, what do you think is going to happen? You killed two of their US operatives, for Christ's sake. You cancelled their ransom leverage when you saved our little topless princess. She's back in Saudi Arabia now and of no further benefit to them. Then you killed the bastards! You fuck with them like that, and you think they won't notice? Not bloody likely, is it? No, Jake, I'm very much afraid they will come after you with a vengeance.

They may be on their way here already, who knows? I should think that would be your focus, not so much worrying about any bent CIA agents we may send your way."

Well, shit. Since you put it that way.

But he wasn't done.

"They will come to kill you, you understand. They don't want to talk or negotiate or sip frozen rum drinks by the bloody pool. You're the target. Govern yourself accordingly."

Reality can be a cold, harsh awakening. Like splashing ice water on your face on an early chilly morning. I leaned back in my chair. Let it all sink in. I was trying to fathom how they may come at me. So I asked.

"How will they come at me?"

Maggie picked that up.

"Interesting you should ask that. We've considered that as well. We assume that these rogue CIA elements are more of an analytical group or intelligence gatherers rather than covert in-the-field operatives. Or maybe they're just printers. So we suspect they most likely aren't accustomed to wet work or that kind of field craft. However, you're an ex-cop and have experience in covert undercover operations, and you are accustomed to a little wet work from time to time. So you may very well have an advantage over them in that regard. And we don't know how many are in this crew, either, but it's not likely there's more than a half dozen. Remember, they run a currency printing operation. They're not really in the threat mitigation department."

That was slightly encouraging. But me against six or so hot-dog CIA-trained intelligence analysts still didn't make me warm and fuzzy. It wasn't optimum odds.

"But what about the Brotherhood? Do you think they will try a hit as well?"

Rup was silent as he pondered that one. Paced around the

office some more. I looked at Maggie. She just shrugged.

"Not likely, I would think. First, the CIA contacts will warn them off because they're too high profile. A Muslim gang roaming around Clearwater will stand out like an alligator in a koi pond. And secondly, I'm sorry to say, they'll probably consider you a limited threat to their operation. Merely one that just needs to be silenced. So I think you'll not see any Muslim assassins hiding under the bed."

That was somewhat of a relief. They may be coming. They may not be. Lovely. But I got the impression he was simply trying to placate me. To put me somewhat at ease. My instincts were telling me otherwise. I knew his reassurance was bullshit. They most certainly would come. And come hard.

Rup picked it back up. He was the planner, it seemed.

"So our job is to infiltrate this crew or otherwise be in the right place at the right time when they make the transfer of their next tranche to whoever is their client's contact. We expect that to be Muslim Brotherhood players, but it may well be others. It may even be CAIR so that there is a perceived level of civility involved. CAIR is a front group, as we are very much aware, but they have a little more viability in political terms than does the Brotherhood. We hope it's the former, as they have the most reach and influence in the radical Islamic world. And taking them out, if necessary, would be more, how shall I say, covert than dealing with CAIR out in the open, wouldn't it? Nevertheless, we take them down and end the connection right there. If we get the big fish, the little fish will, of course, stay little. Or be eaten by other bigger fish. Or merely die off. Either way, they'll have far less influence."

Oh. That's easy. End world Islamic terror with nothing more than an older British gentleman and a beautiful American female. By cutting off their funding source. But that counterfeiting operation in Dallas was only one source. Just one of probably dozens more. Well, at least eliminating one source of covert funding for terrorism had to be a good thing.

If it were up to me, I'd just kill them all. But it wasn't.

Rup looked at me and continued.

"And as stated, your job is to stay here and draw some—or possibly all—of their attention to you so we can expose them. Divide and conquer, as it were."

He paused. Looked me in the eye.

"And you are hereby duly authorized as an active operator within the task force and, as such, the use of deadly force is authorized."

He looked over at Maggie.

She nodded her acknowledgment. Decreed and witnessed. I was sworn. He nodded directly at Mr. Kimber on my hip, then he looked back at me.

"You'll have arrest powers if need be but, Jake, understand this. This is a shoot-to-kill operation. Use extreme prejudice. This operation is categorically terror related. No quarter is to be given. We want them dead. Are we clear on that?"

I just looked at him. What do you say to that anyway?

I nodded.

He looked at me hard to see what impact that minor revelation had on me. I held his gaze. He looked again at Mr. Kimber.

"Nice piece, the Kimber. Technically MI5 isn't officially issued firearms, but as a joint task force operator, I carry the Sig Sauer P229 chambered in .357, the same as the Secret Service issued firearm that Maggie carries. Fine weapon as well. Oh, and Jake? You do have a vest, don't you?"

Yeah, I have a vest. It chafes in the humid Florida heat. So it spends its days hanging in the closet. I wasn't looking forward to personal close-quarter combat.

Mr. Brain wanted to throw up.

So did I.

There was silence in the room for what seemed like forever. I guess we were all running through the scenario in our minds. Mentally playing out our individual parts in this staged play.

I know Mr. Brain was. How do you prepare for an almost certain assassination attempt on your life? How do you psych up for that? It goes well beyond a simple lock and load mentality. And I had other people in my life I had to protect as well.

Dress rehearsal was all but over. Time to get ready for show time.

Rup finished his drink and set the glass next to Maggie's empty one on my desk. I needed a bit of levity after all this spook versus spook talk.

"Well. Does this little operation of ours have a name?

"Of course, old sport."

I had to throw out a suggestion.

"How about Operation Bogus Bill?"

Rup spun to look at me. A slight smile on his face. His eyes seemed to shine with the excitement and thrill of it all. He was clearly enjoying this.

He leaned on his knuckles over my desk and looked me straight in the eye.

Paused for effect.

"Operation Bob Dylan's Belt!"

Jesus.

I tossed back the rest of my drink.

CHAPTER NINE

After Rup and Maggie left the office, I sat down. Hard. Alligator boots went up on the desk. I had to process this new situation. Very exciting. But very goddamn dangerous. Had to plan my defense. Make sense of an unimaginable tangle of events. A gnawing realization began to dawn on me. If they come after me, they'll probably come at me at the house. That's because it always makes a point. Hit where vulnerable. If they come to the house, Rebecca Lynn will surely be in harm's way. Even if they come to the office—or even the houseboat—they could use her to get at me. Abduction. Hostage. Shit. It was starting to become an even more troubling day.

I knew Rebecca Lynn would be in court all afternoon. I couldn't tell her about the recent revelations. Didn't want to worry her. And I didn't need the inevitable ridicule. She usually carries her Kimber Micro 9, being a lawyer and all, but it's in her purse. Not on-body. Hard to get to quickly. And weapons are completely verboten in a courthouse. So she's vulnerable then. And she's there a lot. She's a good shot when we go to the range, but that's a stationary target. Nobody's shooting back. She's not trained for the high stress, panic, and mental failures that everyone experiences when in a gun battle. So

I have to keep her out of this one. Maybe send her back to Chicago for a week or so to spend with her sister.

Things were looking bleak.

I had to pick up Mr. Taylor and center myself. It was time for some six-string therapy. A few minutes—or longer—of jamming solo would help clear my mind of all these spy-versus-spy international intrigue spook games that were going to get somebody killed. Probably me.

Mr. Brain wasn't too keen on that scenario.

Mark-boy.

Maybe even Frank.

I called Mark-boy.

Mark-boy picked up on the third ring. That was a good sign. First, it meant that he was conscious. Second, he was accessible. I opened with a question.

"How's that adventure coming along?"

"Which adventure?"

"The only one I'm aware of—the put-on-your-sailin'-shoes Grand Bahamas Adventure. Are there more?"

"Oh. No, I forgot about that. I thought you meant in a more metaphysical sense."

Huh. This was interesting. Mark-boy was often reflective, but this was the first I'd heard of this new twist. And he rarely if ever waxed philosophical, let alone metaphysical. He must have had his heart broken by some lovely sweet young thing. At least with Mark-boy, that would be only a temporary setback.

I prompted.

"What do you mean?"

He explained.

"Yeah, the Bahamas thing is kinda on hold. Lost my spark for that one just now. The boat needs some maintenance, not to mention the bottom scraped. And I might need new foresail and staysail battens too. Why do you ask?"

I was about to offer to scrape the bottom for him myself, but he had essentially pre-empted that. He was just dreaming up excuses. As to why the sailing trip was indefinitely postponed. And it wasn't an answer to the question I thought I had asked.

So I just answered the question anyway.

"Well, for one thing—you invited me along. And for two, I may have something you could get a kick out of instead. And help me out at the same time."

Anytime I'm about to ask Mark-boy to put his life on the line, I have to soften it a bit. He took the bait. And perked up.

"Oh, yeah? What's up?"

"Well, I'm on a case, that same one, as a matter of fact, and there may be some bad guys coming after me. More than one, actually. I'm way outgunned. Need another pair of eyes. And at least another gun."

"Jesus, Jake. Now we're getting down to it. What's really going on?"

I dodged that one for now. Jumped right to the close.

"Oh. And there's a better than fair to even chance we might get hurt. Or dead."

He paused.

"Is this some kind of fallout from that shootout you were in?"

"It is."

"Goddamn, Jake. You go from bored to tears one minute to sheer terror the next. Like overnight. Hell yes, I'm in. What's next?"

"Not on the phone. Get your go-bag. We'll continue this elsewhere."

"No shit? You're serious, huh?"

"Very."

I hoped Mark-boy knew what "elsewhere" meant.

It had been a month or more since the shootout but only hours since I learned I was most likely a target for CIA rogues and Muslim fanatics. I had to assume they knew more about their possible timeline that I did. So it was impossible for me to know when—or if—they would come for me. Or how many. Or where. But Mr. Brain was reasonably certain they would hit me sooner rather than later. They had time to plan. To prepare.

But I didn't.

I ran through some possible scenarios of how an ambush may go down.

Anyone who knew who I was would know about the houseboat. It was moored in the municipal marina under my name. Easy to find. The bad guys might already have it under surveillance for all I knew. Anyway, it would not make a good defensive last stand. It was small, constrictive, and had no decent fields of fire. They could get me far easier than I could hit back at them. Scratch the houseboat. Let's not go there, Jake.

Mr. Brain was advising wisely.

Or they could hit me on the road. Traffic hit. Or a drive-by shooting. To do that, though, they'd have to have to have me under surveillance continuously, and that takes manpower and time. I didn't see them as being that organized or with that level of human assets. But I could be wrong about that. Further, that technique relied on near perfect execution to be successful. Things like traffic congestion, red lights, pedestrians in the way, and a host of other uncontrolled situations that could adversely impact the level of success. And there could be a lot of witnesses. But it still remained a good possibility.

I tried a different approach. What would I do if I wanted to assassinate me? How would I do that?

Mr. Brain had the answer immediately.

Home.

I agreed with him. Most likely they'd hit me at the house. It was the one place I would always be at one given time or another. Where I slept. And when I was most vulnerable. And it would make the most noticeable and effective statement. Like don't screw with us or you get dead. And your family. Peachy.

Mr. Brain was getting nervous.

So was I.

I had to get there—home—first. Like right the fuck now. Get ready for when they'd hit me. Harden it. Parts of it, at least. Determine the direction of the enemy's attack. Establish clear fields of fire.

That mental exercise was sobering. Imagining a defensive fortification out of my home really put the danger in perspective. It was like watching an apocalyptic movie. Without the popcorn.

And by definition, making a defensive fortification out of my home would assuredly put Rebecca Lynn in harm's way.

Goddamn it.

I headed for the house.

By the time I locked up at the office and finally managed to get home, it was late afternoon. I was surprised to see Rebecca Lynn's car in the garage. Must have been a light day for her. Or maybe her court case had been dismissed or continued.

I had to tell her about current events. The danger posed. I couldn't just let her be unaware of what may become a life threatening situation. That her home— her sanctuary—could very well become a battlefield. Literally the Alamo. But doing so would inevitably mean a quarrel, then a full-blown fight, probably. Ever since after the Coalition event, when we had an inspiring and rousing intimate session between the sheets, she seemed to be softening in our relationship. More attentive to me anyway. So it seemed. Maybe she realized that our relationship required a little more care and maintenance than she'd been giving it so far. I wasn't sure. I hoped so. But it didn't matter right now. I had to get her to safety. Period. By whatever method or ruse it would take.

But still, she most likely wouldn't accept the fact that there was a considerable risk. That would arise from her habit of always marginalizing me. She had an unshakable habit of always thinking not only that she was right but also that any notion or opinion contrary to hers was simply unworthy of discussion. She would refuse to recognize the potential threat. Downplay it, ignore it, deny it. Then she'd accuse me of over-reacting. Being dramatic. Acting self-important. Of being conspiratorial.

You're just a small-town, semi-retired private eye, Jake. You investigate insurance fraud cases. Nobody's conspiring to kill you, she'd say. No one wants to eliminate Jake Randall. You're just not that important.

Mr. Brain had shared those viewpoints with me.

It was nice of him to enlighten me.

I dreaded the inevitable, but she had to be told. I pulled into the garage next to her car.

Before I got out I paused to collect my thoughts. I just sat there in the Jeep. How to present my case. Hardening myself for the almost certain barrage of ego-deflating verbal abuse. Composing myself for the resistance I was about to meet. I'd go ahead and tell her about the danger. She would assure me I was being overly paranoid. I'd insist. Give her the facts. She'd deny the danger even further. After beating me up for harboring overly dramatic delusions, she'd tell me it was impossible for her to just up and leave her practice on short notice. That argument I could understand. I get it. I was keenly aware of the difficulties regarding her schedule, but this was literally life or death. She'd have to get another attorney to cover her caseload or file continuances with the courts, or something. I had to save her. Get her out of harm's way. It'd end in a fight. I had to be firm, but delicate. I had to find a way to get her out of here. To save her life.

My phone chirped. I picked up on the second ring.

It was Rebecca Lynn.

"Why are you just sitting there in the Jeep? Come on in, silly. I made us a nice early dinner."

I had been deep in thought for longer than I had imagined, apparently. My stomach growled. Mr. Brain got interested. I was stunned. She made dinner. For two.

Well, now.

"Wow. That sounds great."

"Formal dining room in five minutes? You can open that French Cabernet Sauvignon we've been saving in the wine chiller. Oh, and light the candles."

Formal dining room. Not the breakfast nook. French wine. And candles? Well, now. Maybe there was hope for us.

"Ok. Consider it done. I'm starved. On my way!"

This would be the first time in a long time that she initiated a romantic diner. And we would be together. Alone together. I was surprised and thrilled. It was a ray of hope shining on a relationship that hadn't been properly maintained in a very long time. Like a spring shower, her overture washed away the gloom in which I had been indulging. It was more than welcome. Maybe I could convince her to go to her sister's for a while after all. With little or no drama. I hoped so. Or at least somewhere safe.

I stepped out of the Jeep.

The commotion behind me caught my attention. I turned and saw a startling scene taking place just outside and beyond the open garage door.

It was a late-model plain white van, and it was tearing across my front lawn at full speed. Clumps of my perfectly manicured grass flew as the van careened across my front yard. Engine roaring.

It tore through the landscaped planting area. Bouncing up and down like a lion in an attack on a surprised gazelle. Rebecca Lynn's prized rose bushes sailed into the air, red and pink and yellow pedals flying, roots trailing rich black soil behind. I thought I could see a face through the oak canopy reflected off the windshield. A face that was hunched forward over the steering wheel. Eyes wide. Screaming something. A fleeting image seen in a nanosecond. The van's motor was screaming, too, as it launched over my citrus tree and crashed right into the dining room picture window. And continued under full power as it plowed into the house. The noise was deafening. Over-revving engine, plate glass breaking, and concrete block wall being pulverized.

My hand went instinctively to Mr. Kimber.

What I wanted was a second or two to respond to and stop the threat.

What I got was a blinding explosion.

Then total darkness.

* * *

When I woke up, I could sense only bright white light. It hurt my eyes. Pale ghostly images floated through my unfocused field of vision. I floated in a sea of serene senselessness. I seemed to be facing up. It was hard to tell. Mr. Brain slowly came on line. He was supposed to run a diagnostic check. I wanted him to make sure that all of me was still there. And under our control. He seemed to think that most of me was still with us. As consciousness returned, so did pain. Complete and unrelenting pain. It was if I were underwater. Deep. Heavy pressure. I didn't want to look, but my chest seemed to be under an elephant. Or a car maybe. It felt flat, heavy. Sounds could be heard, but they were muddled and distorted. Maybe I was deaf. Or near it. Breathing was an effort. My throat was raw and tight. I hadn't worked down far enough to find arms or legs. Yet. The pain was deep and intense. And unyielding.

My tinnitus was being drowned out by a strange high pitched beeping sound. It was increasing in frequency. It sounded like an alarm and it forced itself into my awareness, such that it was. I felt I should do something about it, but it was too much to take on right now. Mr. Brain was trying to hide under the covers. I hurt. Intensely. I couldn't move. At least I didn't want to make anything move. Shit. Helplessness covered me like a shroud.

My vision preferred the darkness to the intense white light. It was too much to handle. I needed to shut down. Screw whatever's going on out there. I'm buggin' out. I fell back into that comforting sea of serene senselessness.

Somewhere out in the dark ether I thought I heard a disembodied voice.

"He's coming awake."

No, not quite awake. My consciousness was limited to what was inside my skull. I knew of nothing else. I didn't care to.

Mr. Brain peered out from under the covers. He wanted to come back. So did I. Pushing back against the serene sea, I opened my eyes again. Blinding white light greeting me. Again.

Slowly the outside world started to come into focus. And into my awareness. Pain was real. Check. Holy God, was it real. I pressed on harder. Pressed my consciousness to travel down my body. Seeking my chi. Hoping it was still there. I tried to awaken my kundalini. There was a spark, but little else. At least I was whole. But I knew I was damaged. Severely. Arms and legs seemed to be attached and functional. Check. Cool oxygenated air was being forced into my nostrils through little plastic tubes. My head throbbed like a tympani bass drum. My hearing was muffled. I could feel a pulse in my neck. That was a good thing, I thought.

"Ah. You're back with us, Mr. Randall."

I turned my head gently and vaguely saw a tall white lab coat standing beside me. There was someone in it. Everything was out of focus. I blinked. It hurt.

Don't do that again, Jake.

Where the fuck was I, and what had happened to me? I had no idea. I asked Mr. Brain to run an archive search. I had to know. And know now.

"Don't try to speak just yet. You're Ok now and out of danger. You're in hospital. You've been . . . hurt. There was an accident."

Accident? What accident? When? Then Mr. Brain found the tapes in archive. The memory came roaring back and emotionally smothered me. Like standing under a waterfall. Or a crashing heavy surf.

Oh, Jesus! A white van. Tearing through the yard. Hit the house. Went inside the dining room. Blew up. God! Rebecca Lynn?

Oh, holy Christ. Truck bomb! We got blown up! Lab coat must have seen the memory returning in my widening and panicked eyes. And noticed the elevating pulse rate on the monitor.

"Mr. Randall, please stay calm. Just relax."

Relax? How the hell can I relax? Where's my wife? Is she all right? Why isn't she here with me? Let me outta here. I gotta find my wife. I'm gonna kill whoever did this. Goddamn sonsabitches. Mr. Brain was seriously pissed off. Lab coat just couldn't hear him.

Lab coat stepped over closer to the bed, obviously concerned about my heightened state of agitation. The monitor was making curious alarming sounds. Jiggly lines jumped, danced, and spiked their way across its screen. I was redlining, that's for sure.

He reached over to the drip bag that was connected to me somehow. Thumbed a valve. It was the right thing to do.

Mercifully, the room faded into black, and I fell back into that welcoming, comforting sea of serene senselessness. It was dark. It was quiet. Systems shut down.

Mr. Brain pulled the sheets over his head.

I needed to rest. To heal.

But I'll be back.

Oh, make no mistake. I'll be back.

And when I do. . . .

CHAPTER TEN

It rained the day of the funeral. Somehow that seemed fitting. Everyone else was crying, why shouldn't the sky? Mark-boy solemnly pushed my wheelchair along the little walk that leads to the site. It was nice gravel path meandering under grandfather oaks, past gleaming white marble mausoleums that had been here for decades. Clearwater Municipal Cemetery. Past the spot where this all began. Where I victoriously kicked the guns out of the hands of two recently deceased terrorists. How ironic.

I pushed away having any thoughts of karma.

I wasn't supposed to be here at all that day, but they had to bury her. Or what was left of her. And I wasn't going to lie in a hospital bed while they put my wife in the ground. The doctors relented, and I ended up able to attend. I was still on an IV drip, and the back brace and frontal body cast the doctors had me in chaffed and hurt like hell. I was pretty fucked up.

When I had finally regained a state similar to consciousness, the doctors told me about my injuries. And about Rebecca Lynn. They were delicate, but at the end of the day the simple fact was that she was blown apart. Died instantly, at least. No shock, no pain. For her. But for me, I suffered the blast wave, and then the immediate shock wave. Caught some shrapnel, but only superficially. My situation was extensive internal trauma from being so close to the blast. Liver, spleen, lungs, and small intestines essentially went through a blender. Same with a few ribs. The concrete block garage wall helped mitigate what could have been much worse. But not a lot.

When an explosion occurs, there's a blast wave first, followed by a shock wave. A barrier can mitigate a blast wave to some degree, but the shock wave is supersonic and you really want to be somewhere else. It can travel through barriers or clothing. Easily. Shrapnel is formed by what's left of the explosive container, plus whatever else is lying about. Barriers can stop a lot of shrapnel. But after all that, there's a vacuum formed at the center of the blast, caused by instant over pressurization of the air. And when that vacuum fills back up, there's a blast wind that rushes in to fill it. And that wind goes in the opposite direction of the initial blast wave. There's an intense push-pull effect as the explosion occurs that's nearly impossible to withstand, and it all happens in mere nanoseconds. Whiplash on an order of magnitude. And it's really, really hard on a human body. Ask any serviceman who's been in a combat zone.

That's what happened to us. Me and Rebecca Lynn. My internal organs were either bruised or ruptured, and I was going to be driving this wheelchair for a while. The back brace keep my spinal column aligned, and the body cast helped hold everything together and inside my broken ribs. And keep it all inside me. Until I healed. And I wanted desperately to heal. I had unfinished work to do.

Rebecca Lynn was essentially at the center of the explosion. She didn't have a block garage wall to partially protect her. She took the entire brunt of the blast.

Losing a wife is unimaginable, but what pissed me off is

losing her just as it seemed we were getting it back. It being that thing couples have. A joining. A closeness. A trust. Now all that was taken from me. She's gone. I had to start over emotionally. And physically. But I had an edge. A desire to even the score. I would find who did this and I would make them pay.

There were hundreds of people there at her funeral. Her friends and associates, lawyers, judges, and others by the dozens. My friends, too, though in much smaller numbers. It was amazing how one person could bring out so many folks. Reassuring in a way. They all came over to me, one by one, offering condolences, all that. They were sincere. It took forever. A dead wife, a husband all blown up, taped up like a mummy, and wedged into a wheelchair. Couldn't have been easy for them. It sure as hell wasn't easy for me.

Finally the crowd thinned out, leaving just me, the bagpiper, Mark-Boy, and Frank.

We watched the cemetery crew do their job and cover the hole with a tarp. Until the rain let up. And the bereaved left. Then she'd be really and irretrievable gone. Buried in the ground. The headstone had been ordered and would come later. Mark-boy finally suggested that we'd said goodbye and it was time to let her go.

I nodded, but then said,

"I want to go see it."

Mark-boy and Frank looked at each other. The piper, playing respectfully off in the distance, finished "Amazing Grace," saluted us, and turned and left.

Frank spoke first.

"That's probably not a good idea, Jake. Besides, we told your doctors we'd bring you right back. You need rest and attention."

"I wanna see it."

I could sense them looking at each other behind my chair. Trying to decide how to deal with this. Mark-boy joined the protest.

"You can't even walk, Jake. You need to get back to the hospital. Not only that, you're all crippled up. And you look like a fucking turtle with all that shit on."

Oh, that did it.

I stood up, hands on both arms of the chair. The drip bagged rocked on its hook. The brace and cast added weight. I was top-heavy. Legs wobbly, but I stood on my own weight and let go of the chair. I turned unsteadily. Looked them both in the eye.

"Let's go. Drive me by the house. Let me see it, damn it."

I was exhausted just from that. I paused for a beat.

"Then you can take me back to the hospital."

It's funny how people will acquiesce to a blown-up cripple. Even when he's probably wrong. Mr. Brain needed me to sit down. Right now. He was getting a little light-headed.

Both men sighed in resignation, and Frank said,

"All right. But sit your ass down in that chair."

I was glad to do just that. I had stood for about a half a minute and it was exhausting. But being that physically diminished just made me mad.

And mad makes me stronger.

Mark-boy had rented a special wheelchair accessible van. They rolled me back out of the cemetery and opened the rear doors. The lift whined as it raised me to the van's deck height. Frank and Mark-boy rolled me inside. Secured the chair to the deck. I still had good visibility out the huge side windows.

My anxiety peaked as we turned onto my street. Seconds later Mark-boy slowed and stopped in front of what used to be my house. Or, more accurately, Rebecca Lynn's house. I thought I might throw up or maybe pass out when I saw the damage.

Yellow crime tape all over. Boarded-up windows in my neighbors' houses where their windows had been blown out. Shredded trees, flattened landscaping. Not pretty anymore. The charred and twisted frame of the van, its rear axle twisted upward in an agonizing angle. The outside of the house, where the hole was, was charred a sickly black. Like the gaping mouth of Satan. The dining room, kitchen, and living room were simply gone. I could see the burned trunks of my trees way out in the back yard. Through the house. My home office sat above the dining room, and it and the whole the second floor sagged precariously. No matter where Rebecca Lynn would have been anywhere downstairs in the house, there was no hope for her survival in that massive blast. Frank and Mark-boy had seen it before, but they still wore somber expressions as they reevaluated the damage.

I looked at the garage. The garage wall was gone, just a pile of busted up concrete blocks scattered around. My Jeep was pushed up against her Mercedes, and both cars were smashed on the blast side. Covered in bits of concrete and dust. Windows blown out. Charred.

Frank and Mark-boy just watched me take in the grisly scene. Then just looked at each other. There was no reason I should have lived. Not through that. Not where I was.

Mark-boy explained the series of events.

"After you told me to meet elsewhere, I ran by my house and grabbed my go-bag. Got my weapons and all. But by the time I got here, it was all over. I was the one who found you in the driveway, and called it in. You were a mess. Blood was coming out of your ears and mouth. Your shirt and jacket were shredded. The side of your chest looked like it been run over by a truck. You were flat on that side. I got one of your lungs inflated and got you kinda breathing, all wheezing and gasping. You were still unconscious. I thought you were gone."

Christ. Thank God I was unaware of that. I shuddered.

Frank picked it up and broke it down for me.

"Why you weren't vaporized is by the grace of God, most likely. Had to be. Pure and simple. Forensics thinks you were blown against the Jeep as it compressed, then sucked back out into the driveway. The Jeep was being pushed back, too, and it absorbed a lot of the blast wave. You were thrown around like a rag doll. Didn't fully absorb the shock wave. Fucking lucky."

Lucky? You call this lucky? Frank immediately caught his faux pas.

"Oh, shit. Sorry, Jake. You know what I mean."

"Yeah, I know. I know. You're right. I probably was."

It sure seemed God had a plan for me. Seeing what was left of the house, and burying Rebecca Lynn did more to strengthen my resolve than months of psychological and physical therapy. I would get well, get strong, and I would find and kill those savages responsible. In the most excruciating way possible. And with extreme prejudice.

That wasn't just an idle threat. It had become a covenant with God.

Three weeks later they took the cast and back brace off. It felt like slipping off a full battle pack. Damn things weighed about fifty or sixty pounds. I was thinner, but taller, and I needed to get my strength back. And I still needed help with the pain.

I headed for the office.

Frank and Mark-Boy and some of my neighbors went through the house right after the forensics team left and gathered up what was left of my valuables. They put all the furniture and personal effects here into one of my vacant office suites. What was still whole and not too badly charred anyway. I did a visual inventory, then closed the door and locked it. The other stuff went discretely to the houseboat. That included my guns and ammo and the safe with my money and jewelry. Mark-boy knew where to hide stuff like that on boats. Marie stayed on top of the books and managed my income and expenses while I was incapacitated.

Rebecca Lynn believed in insurance coverage. Lots of it. So there was an insurance policy on the place that covered odd non-act-of-God events like terrorism or random acts of violence. It was ironic being interviewed by the insurance company's adjuster. Me—an insurance fraud detective. He knew who I was. What I did. He must have felt bad, seeing the photos of the house and of me all blown up and in a wheel-chair, because the claim sailed through. They could have easily argued against the terrorism clause, because that fact hadn't been determined, but they didn't. Out of sympathy or empa-thy, I don't know. Unusual for an insurance company.

I figured the Muslim Brotherhood was behind this. It looked like their work. Car bomb. Savage. Brutal. And very public. It didn't seem to be CIA-analysts-turned-counterfeiters as Rup had predicted. They must have thought they got me too. Or maybe they thought the message alone was enough. I doubted that last scenario. But either way I hadn't had any more attempts on my life. So far.

And I hadn't heard anything from Maggie or Rup, and I seriously wondered about that. Did they know about the hit? Were they so deep undercover that they couldn't risk making contact with me? Were they even alive? I didn't know. I had to assume no one in the Brotherhood knew that I was still alive. That may be an advantage.

I headed for the houseboat.

It was a comfort to open the slider and be greeted by the familiar smell of salt air and bilge. The gentle rocking was soothing and welcoming. I checked the secret compartment in the bulkhead and found where Mark-boy had stashed my

Kimber. It was there along with several loaded magazines and my holster. I grabbed all of it. I slammed a magazine into the piece and racked the slide. Flipped the slide safety on. I slipped the paddle holster onto my belt, and gingerly lay down in my bunk.

The thought occurred to me to have a drink, but Mr. Brain really didn't want one. He needed to heal, and I needed to get strong to right this terrible wrong.

There'd be time for drinking later. Just not right now.

I was exhausted from the simple task of just getting around from my office to the houseboat in my rented Tahoe. I was sore, I ached and, thankfully, I dozed off.

My body was healing, but wasn't yet optimal. My chi was returning, and I could feel its strength increase ever so slowly.

Mr. Brain had been bounced around inside my skull. He was bruised and needed time to rebuild and revitalize the neural pathways in his control room. It was a time to lay low. But vigilantly.

I've heard it said that inspiration can come to a man in mysterious ways. My inspiration blossomed like a giant sunflower smiling at the sun on a hot July day. The resolve to take the fight back to the worthless scum who did this would be my driving cause. There would be an answer to their vicious act.

I'd have my revenge for Rebecca Lynn.

Jake Randall will be back to finish the job.

You can bet on it.

I slipped into a natural, non-drug-induced deep sleep.

I needed it.

CHAPTER ELEVEN

I had a dream. It was unsettling, but it seemed to contain a message. I was on Clearwater Beach Memorial Causeway, headed east back to the mainland. The bridge was unusually high and steep, and as I got to the top, I could see that the center span was missing. The bridge just ended. It wasn't connected to the other side. Only a rickety wooden plank lain precariously between the spans offered any way to get across the gaping opening and back to the mainland. And it was a couple hundred feet straight down to the water. Other people seemed to balance their way across, nonchalant and unconcerned. I balked: a dicey plank, a long fall. Wasn't gonna do it.

I woke up frustrated.

Barriers can be overcome. Obstacles can be surmounted. But how do you bridge a yawning gap? I knew the dream had something to do with my desire for revenge. But it wasn't a stop sign. A yield maybe. Or caution, slow curve. It seemed to be telling me that there was no way to that goal except to cross over that rickety-ass two-by-twelve plank. I needed bravery and trust. It was like one of those ancient epic Greek myths. Homer. Odysseus. Bravery and trust. Lovely.

I wanted an update on Operation Bob Dylan's Belt. I knew

what happened to the bait. It got hit. Hit like a hungry kingfish will hit a trolled mullet strip. Hard. But what was the status of Maggie and Rup's endeavor? I didn't know. Worse, I had no way to contact them. They were deep undercover as far as I knew. I had to wait for them to get to me. If they were still alive. Or maybe they knew about the hit and just didn't care about my situation. I was expendable. Just used bait. Toss it overboard. I had no way of knowing for sure. I pushed the thought away.

"Permission to board."

Mark-boy announced his presence. It was a welcome reprieve from my dream analysis. God knows I'd done enough of that lately.

At least this time it was my own dream.

"Hey, Bud. Come on in."

He stepped through the open slider aft of the cabin. Eyed me up and down.

"Well. You're looking a lot better, I must say. A little gaunt and in dire need of a tan but, on the whole, a lot better."

I acknowledged his assessment. It was encouraging. Shit, even I barely recognized the guy I saw in the mirror.

"I brought us some lunch. We can eat while I bring you up to speed on some things."

That's a switch. He usually hits me up for a drink. Today he springs for lunch. He reached into a large bag and set a bucket of fried chicken and some coleslaw on the table in the galley. That got my attention. Now for me, fried chicken and coleslaw is comfort food. And he and I both knew I needed to eat something real. And I sure as hell needed some comfort. We both slid into the galley's booth and surrounded the helpless crispy chicken.

"Been thinkin' . . ."

Mark-boy paused between bites. I looked up. This should be interesting.

"First, I remember seeing that van as I was on my way to your house. I didn't really pay attention at the time, obviously; it was just traffic. But I did see a white van pass me at a high rate of speed and haul ass your way. No markings on it, just a run of the mill work van. From a fleet, maybe. Dark-haired male driver. Dark complexion. Beard. Young, maybe mid-twenties. That really is all I can recollect."

Interesting. Good to know. Or possibly an irrelevant factoid. I waited for him to connect some dots.

"Second, Frank has been conferring with Ralph Hamilton at Clearwater PD, and they've got forensics looking at the remains —uh, body parts—of the driver. What's left of him is still in cold storage down at the morgue. And in addition to that, they're analyzing the pieces of a detonator as well as the explosives signature. That kind of stuff was all gathered right after the explosion. They also want to know what kind of explosives were used. They're looking for a PETN signature."

I looked at him quizzically.

"Oh, yeah. Well, both Semtex and C4 are plastic explosives, as you probably know, and are readily available through military, commercial, and/or the many black markets. Both act about the same way when used in this kind of truck bomb application. And this looks like that kind of blast. It was directed up and out, as opposed to just blowing a hole in the ground. Truck bombs are generally configured like that so that they can maximize damage to nearby buildings and people. Anyway, the only real difference between the two is that Semtex contains PETN, which is a type of chemical explosive agent, and C4 doesn't. Determining the type of explosive will narrow the search for the source. That's what they're hoping for anyway. Then again, it may not."

"Wow. You've been reading up. Impressive."

Mark-boy laughed.

"That I have. And hanging out with Frank and Ralph and those FBI forensics guys, you pick up a lot of arcane and interesting stuff. How about this. Did you know that bomb makers invariably leave a trace of their particular methodologies behind, which is almost like a signature? Like identifying the painter of an unsigned painting can be narrowed down and determined just by his brush techniques or use of color. And this one—so far—is starting to look familiar to them. They think they seen this particular bomb maker's signature before."

Well, now. Mark-boy had indeed learned a lot about terror bombings. Mr. Brain made a note of that.

But I had a more practical and less theoretical question. I needed answers.

"When will they know? About the type of explosive."

He paused for a beat. I guess he was still ruminating about the effective application of explosives.

He shook his head.

"No telling. FBI has all the information they've gathered so far, and they're keeping it kinda close to the vest. Normally the victim's family doesn't get that kind of detailed information. It's too arcane and possibly upsetting, and most people don't know what any of that is anyway, so they simply don't share it. But they may tell you, because you're an ex-cop and a PI and all, but normally all that is kept in the case file. It's FBI's investigation now. But I can ask."

I nodded as I did serious damage to a thigh. We had already killed the wings.

"Third, the van was a rental, and it was one of a business-fleet lease contract. The lessee was a guy named Hassan Mahajir Awad, who just happens to own a couple of halal-only Muslim delicatessens in Tampa. At least it was his credit card that was used."

I looked up. Awad. That name rang a bell, but I couldn't

place it. How could you not remember that name? I put Mr. Brain on the task of finding out.

Mark-boy grabbed a breast and tore into it.

"This guy's been on the terror cell watch list for a good long while. He's on the government's radar. He hasn't really done anything outrageous or illegal yet except spew the usual anti-America hate and pro-Islamic propaganda drivel on his Facebook page. In Arabic, no less. He was on a YouTube video when he introduced a radical Muslim cleric at a sharia rally in Tampa several years ago, and he was spouting all that anti-American bullshit even back then. His restaurants or whatever are actually meeting places for other radical Muslim cell members in Tampa. The restaurants—or delicatessens or whatever you want to call them—don't seem to do much business with anyone other than hardcore Muslim fanatics. And the feds in various alphabet agencies have had their eyes on most of these guys for a while."

Mark-boy paused as he worked through the chicken breast.

Mr. Brain remembered what John had shown me weeks ago back in the office about this clown. Fat greasy dude. Nasty, hateful terrorist. Lovely.

"Most or all of the federal agencies' suspicion of potential terrorism is focused on the patrons of these delis, that is, on the guys that hang out there. Oh, and in two mosques in Tampa, as well. So the feds think there's a sleeper terror cell being developed, trained, and groomed within these locations. Right here in River City."

Mark-boy paused as he continued his attack on the fried chicken breast. I dished out some more coleslaw.

"So now the current thinking is that the driver of your van was possibly a new convert to radical Islam. Young, dumbass gung-ho recruit. A lot of those types have been showing up lately, it seems. FBI told us that most sleeper terror cells actually targets and recruits these kinds of guys. Through the mosques. You know, disenfranchised millennials of both Middle Eastern and Western cultures and nationalities who are usually dumber than a box of rocks and easily influenced. But Frank and Ralph aren't committed to that yet; they just don't know for sure. About the driver, I mean."

He paused to let that information sink in. Peachy. Rented van. Muslim deli owner. Halal foods. Muslim equivalent of Kosher. Not for moderate Muslims. Sleeper terror cell right here locally. Maybe more suicide bombers drivers too. Poor young, dumb bastards, brainwashed and indoctrinated into being the first martyrs in the first jihad strikes in the Tampa Bay area. Get their 72 virgins. Christ. Spewing that idiotic seventh-century savage ideological dogma is what killed my wife.

I started to get really agitated. I felt the back of my neck getting very warm. My face must have turned red too.

But Mark-boy wasn't close to being done.

"Calm down now. Take a deep breath. I'm not done. There's more."

Oh, boy. I tossed the thigh bone. I was beginning to need a drink.

"One curious post was found on this Awad guy's Facebook page. In Arabic. Translated, it says something like 'A blow begs a blow.' It's an eye-for-an-eye kind of thing, I guess. Secret Service thinks it's a reference to you and the shootout you were in."

I looked up.

"Secret Service?"

"Oh, hell yeah, Jake. You're apparently right in the middle of this . . . I dunno, God knows what. This is a national security terrorism case now. It's connected to you because of the bombing and the shootout, and you're apparently connected to a counterfeiting ring. And counterfeiting brings in Secret

Service. And a bunch more agencies."

Yeah, it sure does. That's how this whole fucked-up mess started. Just my luck I had to go and shoot some sand monkeys and get involved in all this. Trying to be a hero and save the girl.

Mr. Brain reminded me that no good deed goes unpunished. He was right. Again. And then have Maggie set me up as bait in a counterfeiting sting. Bob Dylan's fucking belt and ten thousand illicit dollars. I was set up, conned, and nearly crucified.

Mr. Brain commented on my naiveté. It was nice of him to point that out.

Well, there it was. No point having regrets. I was in it ears deep now. And there are some more folks who were going to be killed. I guarantee it. And it ain't gonna be me.

"And fourth, the house is gone."

I looked up again.

Mark-boy paused as that sank in.

"Public hazard, the building department said. Structural integrity compromised, the engineers said. Neighbors were starting to bitch, city council said. Loudly. City came in and leveled the house two days ago. Trees are still there for the most part, but now it's just an empty, freshly scraped lot. Cars are gone too. Your insurance company will put it up for sale once title gets cleared. Which could take a while.

"And the city will probably bill you for the demolition too. Heartless bastards."

I just nodded. What can you say to that anyway? It was just ruble. It had to be cleared. To everyone else, it was an eyesore that needed to be gone. Cleaned up. Forgotten.

To me it was the end of a long chapter of my life.

I sat back in the booth with a deep sigh. Mark-boy just looked down.

I pushed it out of my mind. I had other matters to contend with just now. The moment passed.

I wondered how much Frank and Ralph actually knew about the task force—Rup and Maggie. And I wondered if Mark-boy knew about that too. Well, there was plenty of intel being shared about this op already, so I decided to keep the Maggie-Rup-Jake triad on the down low. For now.

Meanwhile, Mr. Brain needed a drink. Right now.

I turned around and pulled the bottle of Jack Daniel out of the boat's cupboard. Mark-boy saw the move and grinned.

"Don't do that."

I turned back around and looked at him.

Turning, he reached into the bag next to him on the seat that the chicken came in. He pulled out a six pack of Seven-Up and a fifth of Gentleman Jack and set it on the table.

"I wasn't gonna introduce this unless or until I was sure you were gonna have a drink. Just, you know, in case you were on the wagon or something. Didn't want to instigate anything. And besides, you told me next time I came by to bring a bottle."

I had to laugh.

"Ah. Good move. And thanks, by the way. That was very thoughtful. On both counts."

He just grinned. I finally smiled. He poured us each a mixed drink. I took a long pull and relaxed. So smooth. A familiar act in my now very unfamiliar life. It was reassuring.

And it tasted good. So did the chicken.

"So what's the next move? Your next move? Where do you want me?"

I didn't know the answer to that and told him so. Yet. Had to think it through. But it would start with getting this Awad out in the open. Awad. Jesus. What kind of name is that? I wondered if he knew what that meant in English slang. He was obviously the money man. Muslim Brotherhood member, no doubt. That organization had tentacles on its tentacles. That's OK. Let the government agencies watch him, record him, monitor him. Like they did with the Cosa Nostra—the Sicilian mafia—in Tampa years ago. That's fine. That's their job. It's also less than productive. My job, however, is less diplomatic. I'd make him make another move on me. Get him to act. Then I'd react. Only this time I'd be ready. And I would kill him. It was just that simple.

I looked at Mark-Boy.

"You don't have to get involved, you know. You've done enough. And I appreciate it. And things from here on out could get, well, really hairy."

Mark-boy looked at me like a whipped puppy.

"Get serious, Jake. I already signed on. I'm in and I'm staying in."

I didn't doubt it. I knew he had my six. I just nodded.

Trust and bravery. It was there.

Trust. That was one down.

Now I just had to find the bravery.

CHAPTER TWELVE

The thing about terrorism is that in order to be effective, it has to be random, unexpected, and brutal. The Islamists have it down to an art form. And Mr. Brain had been taking notes. He formulated a plan. He liked it. And it was beginning to grow on me.

I had missed most of the early stories of Rebecca Lynn's demise. Local news and TV coverage of the event was thorough. For the local networks, it was a big news story: local family targeted by a truck bomb. But I was laid up during that time. Heavily sedated during my convalescence. Bones, organs, and a certain psyche had to rest, to heal. I wasn't following the news during that convalescence. Hell, I wasn't following much of anything.

But David and John had made copies of the TV spots and had clipped and scanned news articles for me. Saved it all. I guess they knew at some point I'd want to see how it was covered.

I did.

I was in the office pretending to do some work when they came in. I had been trying to find something meaningful to do. Marie was there bringing me up to date on the bills and deposits. John was his usual reserved self, but David was agitated. Which was unusual in itself. David generally was unmoved by things political.

"Jake, we compiled all the media coverage we could find about your—uh, situation—but every time I watch it, I get pissed off all over again. Goddamn fuckin' savages!"

Marie shot him a look over her glasses.

"Oh, sorry, Marie. But how can you not get enraged over this?"

"Down boy, down. I'm sure it's all very distressful for all of us. But do rise above your passions, David. My goodness."

Marie could melt Antarctica. Cool. Reserved. Always under control. The lady had class. Big time. David just nodded sheepishly and handed me an external hard drive.

"Everything we have is on that, right up to and including stuff that came out this week. Today, in fact."

"Thanks, guys. This is above and beyond."

John jumped in to describe the hard drive's contents.

"This is a 128 gigabyte USB drive. You're gonna want to watch it. All of it. There's stuff in there you may not be aware of. News articles in the general media, opinions in op-eds, some bloggers' positions and their take, video clips, images of players. Like one clip showing CAIR going public, trying to paint Awad as a victim. This from the known pedophile Amir Shelby, no less."

John paused and looked at me but addressed Marie as he continued.

"He was charged with pedophilia and some other things but managed to evade indictment, remember? And there's another follow-up story about how the FBI and other unnamed entities investigated this guy Awad, his radical mosque, and a bunch of his inner circle. His connection to that radical cleric Rashid al-Mubarak has been scrutinized as well. He's heavily connected to Muslim Brotherhood as a major player in that, they think. He owned—well, leased—the van and others, but you probably know that. And there're some follow-up articles about your shootout with those guys in the cemetery. But the best one is the perp walk when Awad was detained, taken to Hillsborough County Sheriff's office, and questioned by FBI and Homeland Security. He's really a slimy, greasy-looking fat dude."

John's recital meshed perfectly with the germ of a plan that Mr. Brain was proposing. It was brilliant, bold, and I no longer cared if it even worked. I took the thumb drive.

"Thanks, guys."

I put the external drive on my desk. Reviewing its content would be something I'd do in private. That would be done later. Marie picked up on that.

Marie reached over the desk and squeezed my hand. Gave me one of her sweet smiles. Looked me in the eyes. She can smile with her eyes too. Everything she wanted to say to me came out loud and clear with that one look. And I noticed. She noticed I noticed. My return eye contact told her I knew. I appreciated that sentiment more than I could ever express.

Then she gave the boys one of her looks and took charge.

"Come on, boys. Let's give Jake some privacy and a chance to review that."

She looked back at me.

"We'll check back with you later, dear. And don't despair over whatever you may see there. Have some faith. I know your strength."

Then she looked at me and smiled again. Patted my hand. The boys picked up on that, and the three of them left my office and me to my privacy.

I plugged the external drive into my laptop. And began the show.

It was grueling, reading and watching it all over again. Especially the early stories I missed when I was laid up and sedated. But the later stories all centered on the politics of Islam. Uncovering a local terror cell network. Possibly. Profiles of the guys I shot in the cemetery. Identity of the driver of the van. Victims. Dead local attorney. What was the real connection to her? A victim of a missed target? In trying to get to me? But there was no victim label for her. She was regarded as mere collateral damage, simply not worthy of anyone's sympathy. She's just a white privileged criminal attorney. Prosecutor of the underprivileged, the underclass, and the forgotten and disenfranchised. Defender of the patriarchal status quo. Wife of the shooter, who mercilessly killed two innocent Muslim boys. She got her just comeuppance. No sympathy for her. Typical media slant. Pissed me off all over again.

And, as news outlets will do, speculation and innuendo was rampant.

What got my attention was the focus on Awad. And on the Council on American-Islamic Relations, or CAIR. No mention of Shelby's perverse sexual proclivities. Spinning Islam being innocent. Of not playing a role in the attack on a local attorney. On the indignation. And the arrogance. And the lies. Indignation that such a well-respected local businessman and a Muslim, no less, could possibly be a suspect in a covert terror cell. That gem from the St. Petersburg Times. Not especially surprising from the far, far left local newspaper. No one in the law enforcement community had actually come out and said that he was a suspect. The Times just wanted to nuke that from the start. Just in case.

The slant was infuriating. The back of my neck was getting warm again. But I scrolled the mouse and read on.

The law enforcement community was being diplomatic. That means politically correct. Didn't want to overstate any suspicions. Or anger or alienate a sizable segment of the local Muslim community. No accusations have been made. No charges have been filed. No arrests have been made. An investigation is ongoing. Can't comment further.

But the implication was clear. It was an unmistakably a premeditated Muslim terror attack on a private American citizen. On American soil. Unprecedented. Not a public target. Not targeting a crowd. Private. The press danced all around it. Tried to present it as merely a vendetta between private citizens. Law enforcement wanted to say the terror word but spun it as motivation unknown. But they all knew it was a Muslim hit. The driver was finally identified as an illegal alien from Somalia. Unpronounceable name. Who cares anyway. Smuggled into the US through Mexico. Was met by operators in New Mexico and assigned to Awad's terror cell in Tampa. He was definitely a Muslim by his own admission on a YouTube video he made before he blew himself up. Along with Rebecca Lynn and me. How he was fighting jihad for Allah. For the glory of paradise. A Muslim hit. I knew it, and every viewer who saw this news segment knew it.

Jesus Christ. What savages were these adherents to Islam.

I considered the whole scenario as a whole for a moment. Diplomacy aside, it was simply a planned and executed act of revenge for two of their cell members being killed in a gunfight. A gunfight that had nothing to do with belief systems or politics or anything other than a forcible rape being stopped. A simple street crime perpetrated by viscous thugs. Stopped by me. But it seemed unimportant to the media that at the time those guys were killed, they were in the process of committing a capital crime. A forced abduction and rape. And it was stopped by an armed private citizen. There was no political element involved. No bigotry. No cultural bias. None. I didn't know they were Muslim terrorists, I was just stopping a crime. And defending myself.

But the press ignored that fact as they pushed the so-called Islamaphobia angle. Now my blood pressure was up, and I was in danger of becoming seriously pissed off.

But I continued to read.

And the germ of Mr. Brain's idea began to bloom.

In two days, Mr. Awad and CAIR and their lawyers would be making a public televised statement in front of the court-house at noon. To hold hands and sing "Kumbaya." Some kind of public relations damage-control stunt. To promote the community coming together. To denounce Islamaphobia. All the usual bullshit.

But not to denounce Islamic terrorism.

And it was at high noon. How apropos.

I picked up my phone and texted a detailed question to Senior Deputy Frank Sanchez, Collier County Sheriff's Office, Naples, Florida.

He replied immediately.

"You sure about that?"

"I am."

A long pause while he pondered my request. I knew what I was asking him. And he knew I knew. It was a big favor. A game changer.

"I'll check."

I leaned back in my chair as I waited for Frank's return. Boots went back up on the desk. I stared at the ceiling fan as I tried to calm down. From reading the deceitful pro-Islamic, far left leaning reporting on Rebecca Lynn's murder. Regulate my breathing. Pranayama. It was starting to work. I could feel my musculature slowly and gently de-tense.

At least there were no phosphenes in my peripheral vision any more. My tinnitus hadn't cleared up much, though.

Five minutes later he was back.

"Yep. Still here."

I let out a long sigh. No turning back now.

I had asked him about a piece of evidence we had confiscated from one of the cartels back in the Glades. It was during one of the last busts we made together. Taken into evidence was a beautiful Lapua .338 magnum rifle with a Leupold scope. A very expensive, high-end, foreign-made sniper rifle wasn't what you'd normally expect to find in a drug gang's arsenal. But there it was. Packed in the same crate as the wrapped-in-coffee heroin.

That's why we kept it.

Well, that was just one reason. The other reason was the high wow factor of a rifle like that. It's basically a military long-range weapon that saw extensive action in Iraq and Afghanistan. That's how we ended up with it. It was part of the heroin contraband we confiscated that comes out of Afghanistan regularly. It was unusual in that it was probably a partial payment or perk for the buyers. When Frank and I busted that flight down in the middle of nowhere in the Glades, we kept the rifle in evidence. But the Dade County prosecutors apparently were not aware of its existence, so when they requested the case's evidence surrender, it was not on the list. In a matter of law, it simply didn't exist.

They never asked for it. We didn't volunteer. We just kept it. Locked up in the evidence room.

It's designed as a military long-range sniper rifle, but it is also serviceable for use as a big-game hunting rifle. Not for elephant, Cape buffalo, or rhino maybe, but certainly suitable for the next level of big game below that. And for human game.

A one-shot stopper.

But because that Lapua .338 magnum round shoots straighter, farther, and flatter than a .50 caliber, it was favored by military snipers. And it still is. Especially by Navy SEALs.

With a muzzle velocity of somewhere in the neighborhood of three thousand feet per second, it is accurate and precise out to sixteen hundred meters and beyond.

Way beyond. That's over a mile.

And I felt I had a need for it.

"Borrow it for a few days?"

There was a long pause on the other end. I saved him from asking me the question.

"Want to run ballistics."

Another long pause.

The cat was clearly out of the bag now, and Frank could read it like the front page.

I could see him pacing around his desk as he digested what I was about to ask.

He texted back.

"Remember that crab shack on the Peace River in Punta Gorda? When we did the Carlos Ruiz stakeout?"

Mr. Brain ran through his archives to find a reference. It took a moment.

Then I texted in the affirmative.

"On State Road 17? Great food?"

"Be there for lunch tomorrow."

"Done."

The die was cast.

* * *

I got there early and took a booth in the back. It was little before noon. What I wanted was a good stiff drink. What was left of my spleen and liver suggested I not do that. What I ordered was iced sweet tea. Mr. Brain noted the choice.

Good boy. It's not even noon, Jake.

I was running the plan through my head for the hundredth

time when Frank slid into my booth. He dispensed with the usual pleasantries.

"Just what the fuck do you think you're doing, Jake? Are you out of your goddamn mind?"

"Hey, Frank. You're early too. How was your trip up?"

He glanced around. Leaned forward on the table. Looked me straight in the eye.

"Don't fuck with me. What are you planning? You know what you're doing?"

Two questions. I tackled them both.

"I think you know what I'm planning. And yes, I do."

Exasperated, Frank sat back and sighed.

"Ok, suppose you tell me. Just so I have it clear in my mind. You know, for clarity."

"I'm gonna fight fire with fire. Terror for terror. On live TV."

Frank let that sink in. Looked at me for a long moment. In his head he was running through my motivation, means, and opportunity. Like a good lawman. He was looking for resolve on my part.

He found it.

But further, and even worse, he knew he was now complicit. He was involved. A couple years from retirement with full benefits. And a flawless career. About to go rogue. Or abandon a trusted friend and partner.

I hated myself for putting my longtime partner of many years in such an irresolvable position. Mr. Brain was pretty upset about it too.

But I hated the killers more.

Frank looked at me in silence for what seemed like a long time. I held his gaze. Then he shook his head and sighed.

"Jesus H. Christ, Jake."

I just nodded an "amen" to the prayer. We were going to need His help, that was for sure.

"This is the worst thing I've ever done to you, Frank. I know that. It's tearing me up. But big picture, this is something that has to be done. Right here. And right now. And it's not just for me. We have to stop this oozing and spreading evil that no one will even admit exists. That everyone tiptoes around."

My big speech was interrupted by the cute and perky waitress. I had asked her to wait until Frank got there before I gave my order.

"All set? Ready to order? What're we having today?"

We shuffled around and found menus behind the condiments tray on the table. Halfheartedly ordered some lunch. Ordered the first menu items we saw. Gator bites. A side of fried lobster bits. Another sweet tea. Collard greens. Mostly things a cardiologist would recommend older guys like us not eat.

The waitress took our orders. Gave us a curious glace, then smiled and turned away. I guess we were giving off strange vibes.

Frank was still concerned about my plans.

"Give the feds some time, Jake. FBI, Defense Intelligence, and Homeland all have agents working on Rebecca Lynn's murder. Investigations will happen. Arrests will be made. You don't have to save the world yourself. And all by yourself."

He was right in one way. I didn't. But wrong in that I could just let it go. I couldn't. I was neck deep in this op. I was the bait. This bait had gotten pretty chewed up too. But this time the bait was going to bite back.

I leaned forward and spoke quietly.

"It was the federal government under the reign of that Chicago community organizer who imported—forcibly, I might add—these unwanted savages into the Tampa Bay area in the first place. Tens of thousands of them were relocated into Hillsborough County. Over ten thousand more in Clearwater and Pinellas alone. They don't assimilate; they stay in tight Islamic communities. Now because of that, real American people will continue to be raped and killed. That's a fact. We'll be told to just get used to it, that it's a cultural thing. Just like they're trying to do in Europe."

"Now you wanna tell me you actually believe the Feds will come in and clean up their own mess? No way, Frank. That will never happen. This was done on purpose. By design. They'll go through the motions, sure. Face time on TV and comforting quotes in the press. But it'll just be a huge circle jerk. All for show. And you know it."

Frank looked down at his hands in his lap. He was massaging his palms with his thumbs. I'd seen that tell before. He was worried. This scared him.

He knew I was right.

Nobody would even name the beast. Let alone try to slay it.

The lunch orders came, and we ate in silence for a while. The food was good; it was great, in fact. Good old Southern-style comfort food. But the atmosphere was somber. And there was little comfort in the food.

"Look. I know it's a war, Jake, and you've volunteered. You enlisted. Signed up. I get it. And that's admirable. But how are you gonna pull it off? You do this hit, they'll find you, hunt you down, and they'll just flat out kill you. And then the feds will dig you up and kill you again. Just to be sure."

Thanks for reminding me. But he went on.

"You'll be fighting on two fronts, Jake. And remember the SOS rules of engagement? Shoot on sight. No questions asked."

Well, now. That was sobering. He was right. There would be no way out alive for me.

I attempted levity.

"I'm counting on divine intervention."

Frank just snorted. Shook his head.

"That's a pretty cavalier attitude, given the situation."

"I'll take my chances."

"Yeah. And take me down with you."

At least he said it out loud. Right then I knew he was in.

"Look, Frank. You can walk out now, and just forget this whole conversation. Drive back down to Naples. Put it back. Say nothing. No one needs to ever know about this. I know you have a lot on the line. There'd be no hard feelings."

Frank just looked at me for a long time. Like he was considering it.

Hell, he probably was.

Then he sighed.

"Nah. Can't do it. I can't just retire with a perfect career. That'd be too boring. I couldn't live with myself with that. I'll just throw it all away on some stupid fucking heroic last stand against the tyranny of cultural invasion. And you're too old and broke down, you crazy bastard, to pull this off right. Somebody's gotta have your six and save your dumb ass."

Even with the biting sarcasm, I was touched. Hell, I was floored. I choked back a lump in my throat. It was a great sacrifice on his part. He was in. We few. We happy few. We band of brothers.

I wouldn't let him down.

So I told him again all about Operation Dylan's Belt. About the funny money. And the rogue CIA agents funding Islamic terror with counterfeit dollars. Maggie's con and Rup's setup. The MI5 and Secret Service task force. And my part in it. As the bait.

And most importantly, how I was going to get away with it.

It was well into mid-afternoon by the time we finally left the little crab shack. Frank was stunned as the whole thing unfolded. He barely said a word. But I could see the worry on his face slowly giving way to the excitement of a coming battle to be won. Like the old days. Gunfights in the Glades. Bad guys down. Good guys win. But this was bigger. Way, way bigger.

And we were older now. Much older. Mortality was a more prevalent consideration than it was back in the Glades days. When a man thinks of his life and how short it is, he's less inclined engage in the dangerous, life-threatening antics of his youth. He's a little more circumspect. And we certainly were.

We walked out to the parking lot. He opened the trunk of his unmarked car and pulled out a large canvas duffle bag. Handed it to me.

"It has a 5-round box magazine. It's full, but that's all the ammo we ever had for it. I don't know if you wanna qualify yourself on this weapon beforehand, but I certainly would. That means you will probably need to buy more cartridges."

He was right, of course. About learning the rifle. But there was no time. Awad was going to make his televised propaganda statement tomorrow at noon.

Courthouse steps.

At high noon.

A movie was playing in my head. Mr. Brain was watching it. Images of Gary Cooper walking out into the street to face down the bad guys. A one-sided gun fight. All alone. At high noon. To save the town. In spite of themselves. And coming out of retirement to do it. I couldn't get over the irony.

I took the duffle bag. Slung it in the Tahoe's cargo area. No turning back now.

"Well, five will just have to do."

It was my attempt at levity.

There was an awkward moment when the enormity of the conspiracy hit us at the same time.

We just shook hands, nothing was said.

And then we headed back to our respective bases.

In opposite directions.

* * *

There's a new office building going up just down the street from the Hillsborough County Courthouse. It was perfect for my purpose and need. Just a shell of a building, with no interior build-out completed yet. No interior walls, no windows. No construction crews on site.

The owners were waiting for tenants. No leases had been signed. They don't complete the interior build-out until they get tenants' specifications. No tenants had signed leases, so none had moved in yet. It was just a vacant, brand-new, unfinished building. And it was a straight shot down the street.

Mr. Brain snorted at the play on words.

Just before 10:00 a.m. on the day of Awad's public announcement, I made my way up the stairs to the fourth floor of the vacant building. It would become my hide. A canvas duffle bag was slung over my shoulder. I found a stack of gypsum wall board. It would make a perfect riser. The sheetrock was stacked about ten feet back from an opening that would soon be a floor-to-ceiling window. It faced the courthouse. Perfect position. I opened the duffle and pulled out the rifle. Adjusted the Harris bipod that was attached to the forend. Set it up on the stack of gypsum board. Snuggled in behind the stack. Leveled the rifle and sighted it in.

Pulled the bolt back and chambered a round. Safety on. Focused the scope. And waited.

It was about a quarter mile to the courthouse steps where the lectern and the ever-present microphones had been set up. The rangefinder had it at four hundred and sixty-three yards. Just slightly over a quarter of a mile. Not an exceptionally hard shot, but not a super easy one either. I had one chance for a kill shot with this unfamiliar weapon. I was relying on the rifle's famous Finnish precision. On its ability to reach out and touch someone. At a distance. A long distance. And on a whole lot of luck.

And divine intervention.

I had time to wait, and I spent it in a Zen-like state of mind. Lowed my brain wave frequency to an alpha state. Calmed my rambling thoughts, controlled my breathing. Pranayama. Getting in the zone. Focusing on the outcome. Literally seeing the results.

One shot, Jake. Make it count. For America. For Rebecca Lynn.

And for me.

The media was starting to gather. TV broadcast trucks were pulled up to the site. Cables were run out everywhere. It was almost showtime. I focused the scope's reticle on the center microphone and clicked the elevation dial on the scope two clicks up. That would allow for the roughly forty-foot drop the bullet would fall over the four hundred and sixty-three yards it would travel. Windage dial was left unchanged. Crosswind was nil. Humidity was normal for Tampa. High.

I had one shot. Had to be perfect.

Then he came out, waved to the crowd. Hassan Mahajir Awad. Bastard. Coward. Killer of innocent women. John was right. Fat, greasy looking. Hair slicked back. Wearing an open dress shirt and a light blazer jacket. Walked to the mic. Behind him was Amir Shelby, the state CAIR chairman. In a fitted suit. Yellow power tie. Another propagandist and terrorist shill. Perverted fornicator of little boys. And goats.

Awad reached out, adjusted the gooseneck mic.

The time had finally come.

He started to speak. I couldn't hear him, but he was in perfect focus through the scope. His hands were on each side of the lectern. I remembered he would get long winded when he got in front of a microphone. He hadn't gotten himself worked up enough to be too animated yet. So his body was mostly still. I put the cross hairs on his forehead. Just above his shaggy unibrow. If I miscalculated the drop, at least he'd get the hit in the mouth or possibly the throat. Either would be good enough.

Long inhale, slow exhale.

I involuntarily flinched when the rifle fired.

Perfect technique.

I immediately racked the bolt, chambering another round. Found Shelby in the scope just to the left and a few feet behind Awad. The Lapua barked again.

I jumped up, dropped the magazine, and racked the bolt again. Cleared the weapon. The ejected round spun out of the chamber, to the right and onto the concrete floor. Closed the bipod back against the rifle's forend. Looked around and grabbed up the two spent casings and the unfired round. The casings were still hot. Stuffed them, the magazine, the rifle, and my latex gloves into the duffel and ran down the stairs. There was no time to assess the damage. Whether I missed, wounded, or killed, it would have the same effect.

Terrorize the terrorists. Random. Unexpected. Brutal.

Frank was sitting in the unmarked Ford in the empty building's empty parking lot. The engine was running. He popped the trunk lid as just I hit the parking lot in a full run. I ran behind the Ford and in one fluid motion threw the duffel in the trunk, slammed it shut, and kept running. Frank tore out of the lot in the opposite direction.

Mark-boy was waiting a couple hundred feet down the cross street. I was running full speed. If anyone saw me, they'd just think I was running from the sound of gunfire. My hands were clearly empty. No weapons.

He pulled up toward me and I jumped into the Benz. He made a left at the next street, then another left at the first opportunity. Two lefts make an about face. We were headed away from the courthouse.

Mark-boy's face was strained as he looked at me. My ears were still ringing from the gunfire. Lapuas are really loud.

He nodded at me questioningly. Did you do it? I gave him a thumbs up.

We drove casually away from the first act of terrorism against the terrorists. On American soil. And on live television.

Mr. Brain was satisfied with his grand scheme. It had worked. Mark-boy had a shit-eating grin on his face that wouldn't quit.

And Mr. Jake needed a drink for the second time since Rebecca Lynn's murder.

We headed for the houseboat.

CHAPTER THIRTEEN

The result was what you'd expect. Over the next days and weeks it was the usual shock, then feigned outrage from the media sources. Wall to wall. The endless calls for more gun control laws, then for coexistence, then for civility of discourse. Can't we all just get along? Kumbaya bullshit. The actual video played over and over on national and international news networks. YouTube had dozens of uploads of it. Always with the "Caution Graphic Images" disclaimer. It was gruesome, yet it was apparently an event noteworthy enough to be televised. No one had ever killed Muslim terrorists like this on American soil before. Not on live TV. In living color. Not assassinated like this.

And no one claimed responsibility.

Some speculated it was other Islamic factions. Al Qaeda, maybe, or Hamas. Or ISIS or whatever they call themselves now. Terrorists sending a message to other rogue terrorists, I guess. Mr. Brain thought that in itself was pretty funny. The talking head analysts all called the shooting barbaric, uncivilized, but extremely well executed. Had to be Special Forces, they said. Highly trained military operatives, they told us. Some suggested Israel's Mossad was behind it. Other conspiracy theories ran rampant. But they just didn't know from where. Or from whom. It was all just speculation, of course.

But still, I was proud of the high praise. Mr. Brain was proud of the plan. It was his plan. And it had been executed perfectly.

The first shot got Awad just above the bridge of the nose. At that distance the bullet's kinetic energy had turned the back of his skull and brain into goo that splattered all over the lawyers and CAIR staffers who were standing behind him. I was pleased with that shot. In the second or so it took for the bullet to hit Awad, Shelby had turned slightly. He caught my second round in the left temple just in front of his ear. That shot took out the right side of his skull and most of his brain matter with it. It, too, sprayed all over the people standing behind them. The blood, brain, and bone fragments found at the scene were from Awad and Shelby, the two terrorists.

The vomit the first responders found at the scene was a joint product of the CAIR staffers and the brave social-justice lawyers who represented them.

Frank had made it back to Naples two and a half hours after the hit. The Lapua .338 magnum rifle and its half-full magazine was safety back home in the Collier County Sheriff's Office evidence lockup. The latex gloves and the two spent shell casings would never be seen again.

I was the prime suspect, of course. They picked me up at the houseboat. Drove me downtown. I got interviewed by agents from every alphabet agency in the country. Same questions. Over and over. I had my story. I stuck to it.

My motivation was clear—revenge. Everyone knew that. But none of the investigators could establish either means or opportunity. No weapon was ever found. There wasn't enough left of the bullets—after blasting through terrorists' thick skulls—to determine either make or caliber of the weapon. The investigation revealed I owned only an M4 carbine and a 12-gauge shotgun. Neither of those is suitable for making a shot like the ones that took out Shelby and Awad.

And I had a rock-solid alibi. Mark–boy and I were on the houseboat drinking and doing general maintenance all that day. I even paid my slip rent by personal check, in person, to the harbor master. Got a receipt.

Can't be too careful.

Not only that, but I had a get-out-of-jail-free card. I was authorized to use deadly force. Mr. Brain remembered what Rup had told me. He recited it to me. Word for word.

And you are hereby duly authorized as an active operator within the task force, and as such the use of deadly force is authorized . . .

I knew that was a last-ditch defense. First, because it was verbal. And second, the task force was deep undercover, and confirmation of such a decree would be hard to come by. And it would require either Rup or Maggie to attest to its veracity. And that testimony may or may not be readily forthcoming.

But it was there, nonetheless.

So it turned out none of the investigating federal agencies could put together a case against me that they could successfully prosecute. Or maybe they just wouldn't. But I doubted that since there was some serious animosity toward me from the perpetually left-leaning politicos that make up the government. Besides that, Muslims apparently had become a protected class in government circles.

And I had been pretty busy killing them lately.

A curious thing, though. I've interrogated my share of perps over the years, and I can read both sides of the interrogation table like a book. I can tell where an interviewer is going with his questioning. And I can tell how truthful a suspect's responses to interrogation may be.

But with me as the suspect this time, undergoing intense interrogation, I could see something in their eyes. Every single one of the Federal agents who interviewed me knew beyond a shadow of a doubt that I was the triggerman. It wasn't even up for debate. They knew I knew they knew too. But they also knew my back-story going in. A good Samarian stopping an abduction and rape crime. Killing two bad guys and saving a victim. Being targeted by a vicious terror cell as revenge. Losing a wife and home to that insane savagery. Getting blown up and nearly killed in the same hit. I had their sympathy, if nothing else.

But what I saw in their eyes was a grudging respect. Even admiration.

For one guy. One little broke-down, half-assed ex-cop private eye. One guy, who took on the entire Muslim Brotherhood by himself. One guy who stood up. Stood up to the tyrannical bully that the US government wouldn't even admit exists.

So there would be no indictment. No prosecution. Hell, several of them told me outright and to my face that if it was up to them, I'd get a national medal. I was a hero to most of them. Some even shook my hand.

They were envious in a way. They clearly knew what had to be done. To save the country. Save the culture. But they had different rules of engagement. They had to fight a hands-tied-behind-the-back fight with those seventh-century savages every day. And hamstrung by the absurdity of political correctness. And liberal judges. And the bullying media. Yet every one of them would have loved to pull that trigger themselves. It was humbling. But all the same, I had been counting on that kind of brotherhood.

On that camaraderie.

On the kindness of strangers.

On divine intervention.

I guess my covenant with God turned out to be righteous after all. I was alive and healthy. And free. Dharma had protected me. But it cost me dearly.

I guess testicular fortitude—that means balls—is contagious, because weeks later, the FBI and DHS raided two radical mosques over in Tampa. The same ones that Awad and Shelby frequently attended. And where al-Mubarak had given so many radical jihadist speeches.

It was noted that these mosques especially were generating an unusual number of radical anti-American jihadists. The feds arrested the mullahs there along with a dozen or so of their budding jihadist adherents. They were all engaged in subversive anti-American rhetoric. And activities. Out of their minds with rage. Their videos and social media rants proved it. They even had jihad training pamphlets printed up. In Arabic and Farsi.

In the raid, the feds also found small arms, pipe bombs, and both Semtex and C-4 plastic explosives cached there. And primers and timers too. The state closed those mosques as terror cell centers, and the worst extremists are still being held in custody. In Gitmo, probably. Those who were illegal aliens—which was most of those arrested—got summarily deported, family and all.

But not Rashid al-Mubarak. He got away.

Maybe the US and state governments were beginning to shed some political correctness, and actually grow some *cojones*.

About goddamn time.

I was sitting on the fly deck of the houseboat watching the sunset. Thinking about where I would go from here. Spiritually and emotionally, I mean. I had a cigar in one hand and a Jack-and-Seven in the other.

It was time I got some tan on those shrapnel wounds on my arms and chest. Mr. Brain reminded me that scar tissue doesn't tan. Didn't matter, I was determined anyway.

I was lost in thought. Trying to reevaluate the whole Operation Dylan's Belt thing. Trying to tie up the loose ends. Mr. Brain reminded me of the futility of that exercise. Because every operation I've been involved in, and nearly every crime I've investigated, there are always some things that just don't get tied.

But I ran down the chronology anyway.

It was a successful op, I thought. Big picture, the counterfeiters presumably got burned, arrested, and charged. Or maybe flipped. The mosques got raided, and the terrorists got cleaned out. Jihadists were arrested, killed, deported, or otherwise eliminated—for the time being anyway.

But the Brotherhood was still in operation. Still yearning for a global caliphate. And still killing to get it. That still pissed me off.

On the upside, neither Rup nor Maggie had asked for the ten grand in counterfeit supernotes back. I had given one to Nick and another to Sung-Ki. The rest were still mine. Mr. Brain was happy about having an extra nine thousand eight hundred dollars in cold hard cash in the safe. Maybe they just wrote it off. Or maybe it was bogus cash and of no consequence. But I was sure that dough would come back into play somehow. And end up being a screaming monkey gnawing on my skull. Easy money always does.

On the downside, I never did find out who was behind the breaking and entering on my office that night. I doubted it was Muslims. It just didn't fit their typical mode of operation. Had to be spook government agents, I figured, but couldn't make a connection. Nor could I gather whose government would be that interested in a semi-retired, half-assed, broke-down PI.

What the hell could I possibly have that anyone would want? It was a mystery. And that black Suburban is still a ghost.

Not long after all this chaos began to settle, I got a text from Maggie.

Her text told me she was still in Washington, DC, being debriefed. That she hoped to be coming back to Clearwater to brief me in a few days. Or soon. To bring me up to date on the Dallas counterfeiting operation. To the extent she could, of course. It would still—and always be—classified.

And to offer her condolences for Rebecca Lynn. Well, that part I just surmised. She didn't say it outright, but I could tell she felt somewhat responsible. For what happened to me. And to Rebecca Lynn.

How could she not?

At least that's what I read into it. I hoped I wasn't wrong about that. And I presumed she and Rup had successfully cracked that case just from the tone of her text. And the fact that their respective governments are interested in debriefing them on it. I wanted to hear those details too. I hoped there was no more counterfeiting going on. Especially of bogus American cash being funneled to the Brotherhood to finance their nefarious activities.

And especially at the hands of our own CIA, for crying out loud.

And then she asked me if Mark-boy could maybe show her some condos on Sand Key.

Well, now. Mr. Brain thought things were definitely looking up for ol' Jake.

But then again, how did she know Mark-boy was in that line of work?

I let that question slide. She's essentially a spy, after all.

And I really did want to see her again. That scared me. I hoped she was considering a move to Clearwater in part because of me. If that indeed was her intent. But she's a spy, and spies rarely develop roots. Or relationships. Deep or otherwise.

Careful what you wish for, Jake.

A half-hour later, Rup texted me that he had flown back to the UK directly from Dallas to brief his superiors at MI5. He assured me we'd catch up again soon. Maybe get together and jam like in the old days.

Now that we know of each other's existence, old man.

I was still in the glow of hearing from Maggie. Rup's text psyched me up even more. I couldn't wait. It'd be fun. They hadn't killed me. Yet. Mr. Brain was optimistic.

I pondered the events leading up to the last few days. It was time for confession and absolution. The cosmos was listening. Was outright murder something I could live with?

Probably. I'd killed bad guys before, and evil in any incarnation must be stopped. Big outcomes sometimes start with small actions. But I was concerned for Frank and Mark-boy. Accessory to murder is no laughing matter.

I hoped my covenant with God was righteous. I considered it to be that. The dharma was smooth and clear. The universe was in sync. And what the hell, even if that wasn't the case, bad decisions make good stories.

And I may have initiated a save-the-country movement that I hoped was beginning to spread. Americans by nature are mostly self-sufficient, and I hoped they would do what was needed to protect and defend the Republic and the American culture. Mr. Brain wanted the credit for that. He was right. It was his idea after all.

Just don't call it vigilantism, he admonished.

But whatever label you put on it, it cost me my wife and my home. It was a bittersweet victory. Actions have consequences. But I can now start my life all over again.

Maybe take on some more boring insurance cases.

So with any luck at all, the whole bizarre and surreal case of Bob Dylan's Belt would be put to bed. Solved and closed. And after all this time, I was certain I wouldn't be indicted for the double homicide.

Especially since I hadn't been already.

Maybe Mark-boy and I would finally get that Sailin' Shoes Gulf sailing adventure he talked about. I'd be thrilled with that. Get away on the open ocean, away from man and land for a while. Breathe salt air. Cleanse the soul.

If not, it's time to get my normal life back.

And regain my lost tan.

So tomorrow around midday, when I roll out of the rack, I'll go to the office and try to get back to my normal routine. Maybe check my email for any new insurance cases.

Maybe I'll even give Russell Davidson a call. Well, OK, maybe not.

Maybe I'll go sit in with Dave and the Studio Boys at their next rehearsal. Get my blues chops back. And new calluses on my fingertips.

I'll order a couple dozen roses for Marie in thanks for her helping me out when I was laid up. And forgive the rent for a couple months for John and David compiling the media coverage for me.

And for just being there for me.

Then I'll head over to the Fort Harrison Pub after work around shift change.

I'll belly up to the bar, shoot the shit with Mac and Betsy.

Order a couple of Jack and sevens and one of Mac's famous hot-pressed Cuban sandwiches.

And maybe—just maybe—Mac will come up with some bacon-wrapped scallops.